Details

The Red Shoelace Killer
A Minnie Markwood Mystery

by

Susan Sundwall

Susan Sundwall

Mainly Murder Press, LLC
PO Box 290586
Wethersfield, CT 06129-0586
www.mainlymurderpress.com

Mainly Murder Press

Copy Editor: Paula Knudson
Executive Editor: Judith K. Ivie
Cover Designer: Karen A. Phillips

All rights reserved

Copyright © 2012 by Susan Sundwall
Paperback ISBN 978-0-9881944-0-3
Ebook ISBN 978-0-9881944-1-0

Published in the United States of America

Mainly Murder Press
PO Box 290586
Wethersfield, CT 06129-0586
www.MainlyMurderPress.com

Dedication

For Mom,
who believed in and hoped for me
and will be lifting the clouds,
peeking down from heaven,
to see that belief and hope realized

One

"Oh, Minnie!"

Her voice came whistling through my headset, and I yanked it away from my offended ear. "What is it, Rashawna?"

"Wait'll you see this one, Minnie. He's gorgeous." After her initial outburst she attempted to keep her voice low and calm, no doubt because the guy stood close enough to inhale the scent of her dark curls. Probably checking out her curves, too.

"Send him back," I said, smoothing the survey forms on the table in front of me. I waited to interview the gorgeous fish Rashawna had reeled in.

My co-worker, Rashawna Jones, and I work for Chapel Marketing, Inc. In addition to new product promotions, mystery shops and movie theater head counts, we do on-site customer opinion surveys. Today we were in the Roaring Gate Mall in Albany, New York. Our workspace was in a small rental area, a dent in the wall really, about fifty feet from the main mall corridors, and we wore headsets for instant communication. Rashawna covered the floor space at the bottom of the escalators, flashing her smile at potential survey takers, and I administered questions in what we liked to call our little hidey hole. Chapel Marketing had authorized us to pay five dollars to each participant for this particular survey. We'd been hard at it since nine o'clock in the morning, and Mr. Gorgeous was only the fourth person who had succumbed to Rashawna's charms. Those charms worked especially well on males, as she had been a swimsuit model all through high school. With her glossy black curls, killer curves and huge dark eyes, she was fully capable of causing a dog pile of teen boys at the bottom of the escalator.

But today was Monday and a bit slow. For about two seconds I wondered if Rashawna and I had the same understanding of the word gorgeous. I heard her heels click-clacking on the tile floor as she ushered in her prey and motioned him to the chair on one side of the tabletop partition. Considerable research had been done by the good people at Chapel Marketing, who came to the conclusion that survey questions were answered more honestly if there was a partition between the taker and the takee. Today we were asking opinions about a new deodorant soap. Rashawna popped her head over the partition and winked.

"Minnie will be giving you the survey today," she said, turning back to Mr. Gorgeous. She handed me his qualifying questionnaire, which basically certified that the takee was a breathing adult who could spare five minutes for the sake of consumers everywhere. "It won't take long, and I'll give you the five dollars when you're done."

I heard Rashawna fussing with the lavender and peach scented deodorant bars on the table. It was a certainty that she was attempting to convey by flirtatious glances that she would consider seeing him later. I further imagined her sashaying reluctantly away, hoping he would turn to watch her walk. She had quite a nice swing on her back porch, and I had no doubt Mr. Gorgeous was taking full advantage.

"Good morning Mr. ..." I glanced quickly at the sloppily penned name: Ian Kinky. "Uh, Mr. Kinky. On the table you'll see several bars of soap." I didn't finish. Mr. Kinky had apparently decided to live up to his name and have himself a look over the partition. My guess was he hoped to encounter another young beauty on whom he could work his charms. He was green-eyed and fair with a shock of wavy blond hair and solid, even features. His leather jacket squeaked a little when he moved. However, what he said next was a great detraction from his appearance.

"Aw, crud, an old lady," he groaned. He couldn't have sounded more disgusted.

I had no doubt that he was disappointed by what he saw, a woman somewhere between forty-eight and sixty years old sporting short, steel gray hair, generous hips, amused blue eyes and giant silver hoop earrings (one of the three hundred pairs I owned). I winked at him.

"Ah, ah," I said, waving my finger. "No peeking at the lady behind the partition." You see, Rashawna had recently turned twenty-one and was cute as a bug. I, on the other hand, am quite ordinary and just a tad north of a hundred seventy pounds. Perhaps our takee thought Rashawna and I were a double team of cuties. Poor Mr. Gorgeous, he looked crestfallen.

"I am so outta here!" said Mr. Kinky. Why did I think that wasn't his real name? He left my humble hidey hole, and I concluded that he was not my idea of gorgeous.

It was mere moments before Rashawna click-clacked rapidly back in my direction. "What happened?" she hissed.

"My dear, didn't his name send up any alarms for you?" I cocked an eyebrow at her.

Rashawna whipped his questionnaire off the table. "Oh, I thought it said Mr. Kinko," she said defensively. "You know, like the copy place?" She sighed. "I hate this job." She sat in the chair recently ignored by Mr. Kinky and plopped her chin in her hands. "You know, I only gained eight pounds and suddenly, no more swimsuit work. What's up with that?" She cocked an eyebrow back at me.

I was at a loss for a response. From where I sat the eight extra pounds looked great on her. I wondered how many pounds of tofu she'd eaten to gain the weight.

"How do you keep from being bored to death back here?" she asked.

"I read, dear," I answered, picking up my copy of the *Albany Times Union* and waving it at her. "You've heard of newspapers, Kindles and books, haven't you?"

"Oh, yeah, I've heard of them. Don't bother with them much, though." She grinned, and then a sudden thought lit her face right up. "My new guy, Joel, is picking me up exactly at five today. Can you wrap up here? He's taking me to Applebaum's for supper."

"Sure," I said. We both turned when we heard a squalling toddler. His harried mother asked if this was the place for the five-dollar survey. Rashawna got up, smiling, handed the woman a questionnaire and scurried back to the escalators. I motioned the mother over. Her drawn-out sigh indicated her relief at finding a place to sit for a few minutes. I pushed the partition aside, filled out the qualifying questionnaire for her and asked the poor woman the survey questions while she used the table to change her little screamer's diaper. Whew! Talk about needing deodorant.

When Mom and her child left it was almost lunchtime. I retrieved my lunch bag from the one small cabinet available to us and settled in to enjoy my leftover meatloaf and applesauce sandwich, an invention of my own. I shook out the newspaper and skimmed it for content. Buried in the back page of section two was an article with a reference to the Red Shoelace Killer, a case that had bedeviled the Albany police for quite a while now. The victim's mother, Alberta Landis, had just died, not knowing the identity of her daughter Jennifer's killer, and the article included a rehash of the crime. When the story first made the headlines over two years ago, I'd kept up with the case, but coverage died as more sensational fare took the spotlight. There were terrorists and drug kingpins on the loose, for heaven's sake, so who would be interested in the mysterious demise of one young woman?

As it happens, among several other interests in life, I'm an armchair sleuth. For twenty years I worked as an assistant in our local public library, and I'd read every crime-solving mystery I could get my hands on. When my husband died ten years ago, I gave up that position, and after the hassle of selling our home and most of the contents and finding an apartment, well, I got bored. Marvin and I had not been blessed with children, and my sister lived in Poughkeepsie, a good hour and a half drive away. A close friend referred me to the job at Chapel Marketing, and I came to realize it was somewhat like my library job. Both included interaction with an interesting variety of people from the community, and it was low key enough that I had energy for other things and a little income, too. Meanwhile, my interest in crime, in all its fascinating variations, remained keen. Agatha Christie had nothing on me.

I read the article to the end, including the part where police were renewing their warning to all young females, especially those with long, dark hair, stating that they should always travel in pairs and avoid dark parking lots, etc. Possibly there was a belief in the halls of law enforcement that the article would spur new mischief by the heretofore undiscovered killer. If memory served me, the original story had a brief bio of the victim, stating that Miss Landis had been found with a red shoelace tied in a triple bow around her right ankle. She had been strangled with the same shoelace and left partially buried in a wooded area near one of the local high schools. My hand went instinctively to my throat, and I gave an involuntary shiver. Nobody, including family members and local investigators, had come up with a plausible theory for the red shoelace. It was a signature or token of some kind, but of what significance no one ever discovered. Several boyfriends of the beautiful young woman had also been questioned at the time, but again, a dead end. The mother's death notice featured an old photo from the daughter's funeral and noted her two best friends from high school walking behind the girl's parents. It would be interesting to know where those girls were now.

I briefly pondered the red shoelace angle and tried to think of a place in the mall where they could be found, maybe a novelty store or a party warehouse. The thought of a Dollar Store occurred to me, too. They seem to have popped up like mushrooms under oak trees lately. I mentally scribbled a note to self to visit the Dollar Store in the mall right after work. I could accomplish two goals at once. I was all out of my favorite candy treat, Taffy Tails, and sometimes the Dollar Store had them on sale six for a buck.

At four o'clock the time really began to drag. The noise from the corridors had dropped off considerably. I blocked my view of the mall with the partition and picked up the mystery I'd been reading, *The Mirror Crack'd*, a Christie that had recently been featured in a BBC production. But a few paragraphs in, I was nodding. I awoke with a start when I heard a voice. No warning from Rashawna through the headset of any takers, and I was pretty sure she'd gone off with her new guy already.

"Is this the chapel?" It was a tentative male voice, and I shook my head to clear it.

"Yes, come in," I said, trying to put a smile in my voice. "The survey only takes five minutes and ..."

"I got something to confess," he said, all hushed. "I'm glad you can't see me."

Uh oh, another one looking for the other chapel, the one operated by Our Savior's Lutheran Church at the opposite end of the mall. It had been in the mall for almost fifteen years, and there had been recent talk of scrapping the little chapel to use the space for a trendy tee shirt shop. Back in the early '90s shoppers had used it for spiritual sustenance or sometimes help in overcoming an addiction to mall tacos. We got the odd straggler in our area who was looking for it. I began to push myself up from the chair to tell him his error when he quickly spoke again.

"You know that shoelace killer?" he whispered. "I think I know who he is."

I froze. The mall was quiet. It was that time just before the dinner hour when the shoppers headed for home and the teens and 'tweens for the food court. This guy was obviously in the wrong place, but I lowered myself back into the chair as the sleuth in me went on high alert.

I grabbed a survey pen and the clipboard and shoved in a clean piece of paper. My heart became a trip hammer and any insightful, probing questions that might actually help the case escaped me. Think, Minnie! "Uh, okay. First, give me your name. Then tell me what you saw, uh, heard or anything." My hand shook as I poised to capture his words.

"Are you a lady priest or something?" he asked, his voice even more tentative now.

"Well, not exactly."

"Minnie?"

It was Rashawna in my headset. Dang! Her voice echoed down the corridor. The visitor's chair rolled back, and I knew I had to talk fast or lose my mystery man.

"Could you just tell me your name?"

Too late. The guy bolted from the chair and nearly knocked Rashawna over as she entered the hidey hole.

"Hey!" she yelled.

I scrambled up from my seat, knocking the partition over, and burst into a stumbling kind of run, but my attempt to follow him was futile. "Hello!" I yelled at his retreating back. "Wait, please!" I did a quick assessment of his clothing and general appearance. He had on black pants and an oversized tee shirt. His sneakers were new, and he had a full head of dark hair with a bandana tied over his forehead, sort of like Tonto. And, boy, could he run.

"Minnie, what are you doing?" Rashawna's eyebrows were nearly at her hairline.

"Where were you?" I asked, my breath coming in short gasps. I made a second note to self to cut down on the applesauce in my meatloaf sandwiches.

"I ran to the ladies room. It's almost five, and I didn't think it would matter."

"That young man came in to confess," I said.

"Confess? To you? Oh, I get it. That boy had the wrong end of the mall," she said, shaking her head.

"He didn't even give me his name."

"Well, I can tell you that," said Rashawna, hands on her hips and disgust in her voice. "That's my boyfriend Joel." She stomped her foot and glared at me. "Why'd he run like that? He looked like a scared rabbit! What did you say to him?"

"Hardly anything," I said. "You came charging around the corner and spooked him."

"Shoot, now what am I going to do for dinner? I'm dead broke until payday." More foot stomping plus a lip-stretching pout.

"I don't remember you talking about any Joel," I said. "How long have you known him?" I asked warily.

"Uh, well, about three days."

"Three days, and he's your boyfriend already? What do you know about him?"

"Well," she said, a little indignant, "not much. He works at the Dollar Store and ..."

"The one here in the mall?" I interrupted, remembering that I'd wanted to check that store right after work to see if they sold red shoelaces. Crank up the sleuth radar ten notches. What connection was there between Joel, the Dollar Store and maybe the killer?

"Come with me," I said, grabbing her hand.

We returned to our hole. I rummaged around and found the newspaper with the article about the Red Shoelace Killer, folded it and pointed to the column.

"See this? Your boyfriend came in here and told me he thinks he knows who this is."

"Get out!" Rashawna snatched the paper from me and did a quick read. "What'd he say?" she asked, clutching the paper.

"He only had a chance to say he thought he knew who it was, and then you popped in."

"Who did he think you were, a priest or something?" She glanced back into the corridor as if he might be there lurking, looking for her.

"He mistook this for the Lutheran chapel. He did ask me if I was a lady priest, but I think he was so eager to talk that that wouldn't have bothered him."

"Too weird," she said, scrunching her brow. "How could he confuse this place for the chapel?"

"Similarity of the name, maybe?"

"Well, yeah, I guess." Rashawna looked at the newspaper again and read. "This poor girl, it looks like her best friends are in this picture, too. Hey, this is funny."

"Oh?" I leaned in and looked at the picture again.

"These two girls have the same sweater on. How could they do that?"

"Maybe they both hit the same sale," I offered.

Rashawna rolled her eyes. "It's bad enough they had to go to their good friend's funeral, but to each wear the same sweater ..." She shuddered. "I wonder how that went down."

"It's a strange and interesting observation, Rashawna." Third note to self: explore that angle somehow. "Well, it's quitting time, and I'm ready to beat it out of here," I said.

Rashawna handed the paper back to me and got her purse from the cabinet. "I guess I'll shove off, too. Maybe I'll run into Joel out there somewhere. I'm hungry."

I picked up the rest of my belongings and crammed the remaining surveys into the box under the table. I still intended to check out that Dollar Store. It occurred to me that I could also head over to the police station to visit Dan Horowitz. He was an old friend and a great detective. I was sure he would be very interested in what I had to say, and I could at least give him a description of Joel.

Before Rashawna took off in the opposite direction from me, she mentioned going to Applebaum's to see if Joel had possibly shown up there for their dinner date anyway. I headed for the Dollar Store, which was only six stores down on the opposite side of the Chapel rental space. I was in dire need of a Taffy Tail.

Two

The Dollar Store was packed to the ceiling with knickknacks, paper products, greeting cards, candles, toiletries—you name it. Wandering up and down the rows, I eventually found shoe polish, foot care products and shoelaces in the health care aisle. Unfortunately, there were no red shoelaces among all the bubble packs of brown, black and white ones. I had hoped that since Joel worked here, he might have had his suspicions about a customer who purchased red shoelaces. Perhaps one customer seemed to be in too great a need of the things. In the next aisle over I grabbed two bottles of my favorite shampoo and a roll of paper towels, then headed for the candy aisle in search of my Taffy Tails. I'd been addicted to the long, caramel whips with the creamy centers for twenty years, and what luck, they were on sale four for a dollar. Okay, not as good as six for a dollar, but I never missed an opportunity to stock up. I just hoped they weren't too stale.

There were three people in the checkout line ahead of me, and I had a chance to look at all the odds and ends positioned at the point of sale, placed just so to encourage last minute impulse buying. Gosh, those product display people were smart. I noticed a whole selection of cheap kids' toys, including neon green balls, plastic toy boats, birthday party hats and—red shoelaces! There they were, laced into cardboard clown shoes and displayed on a pegged rack along with lots of other party goods. Bingo!

"Do you sell many of the party supplies?" I asked the checkout girl when it was my turn to pay up. I kept my voice casual and congratulated myself on asking a probing question this time.

"Yeah, a lot of them," she said, bored to death at having to actually speak to a customer.

"How about the red clown laces?"

"Maybe," she sighed and shoved my items into a bag. "That'll be eighteen dollars."

Boy, those Taffy Tails really add up. I risked one more question with the most bored clerk on the planet. "Do you know the fellow Joel who works here?"

"I do," she snapped. "That jerk is supposed to have his sorry butt cheeks behind this counter right now. Do you know him?"

"Not exactly," I said, backing up a little. "I know a friend of his." I grabbed my bag and left the store with the clerk's eyes boring a hole into my back. Yeesh, what a charmer she is, I thought as I headed in the direction of Applebaum's. Maybe Joel and Rashawna were having a spicy chili steak with Applebaum's special Tex-Mex sauce, and I could question them while they ate, maybe even join them. No such luck. I described the couple to the restaurant hostess, but she gave me a hurried "Nope," and rushed to help clear tables. The dinner crowd was descending, and she apparently had no time to play Guess This Customer with me.

As I walked through the mall, heading for my car, I did a quick recap of what I was slowly beginning to think of as The Case. The Red Shoelace Killer had been on the loose for twenty-six months. Jennifer Landis, the victim, had been a local college student, working her way through by holding down two jobs. The photo in the paper had been a bit blurry, but from what I recalled she'd been of medium height with long, dark hair and in her early to mid-twenties. Her body had been found in a shallow grave with a red shoelace tied in a triple bow around her right ankle, obviously some meaningful token to the killer. About an hour ago Joel, Rashawna's boyfriend of three days, came into our hidey hole, intending to confess that he thinks he knows who the killer is. Then he jumped up like a jackrabbit when Rashawna came sailing around the corner. The Dollar Store store where he works carries red shoelaces. Again, I thought of Dan Horowitz and wondered if this was enough info to take to him. The only way I'd know was if I paid him a visit.

I'd parked my car in Section H of the sprawling mall parking lot. It was the second week of October, and the sun was low in the sky. I opened the door and threw my Dollar Store bag into the passenger seat. I'd pulled out a Taffy Tail on my way to the car, and as I settled myself behind the steering wheel, I slid the wrapper halfway down. A little something sweet to chew on always helped me think. I took a bite and started the car. As I began to back up, the sun hit my rearview mirror and flashed brightly into my eyes. I fished around in the console for my sunglasses, but as I put them on a dark form blotted out what remained of the sunshine. Someone was in the back seat.

"Drive," said a voice. A gun was pointed at my temple. A thin trickle of Taffy Tail juice slid down my throat, and I swallowed hard. The voice belonged to Joel.

"Ah, so," I gasped, trying hard not to sound scared witless. "Rashawna's told me about you, Joel. That's your name, right? And Rashawna's your girlfriend? She went looking for you at ..." I was beginning to gabble.

"Huh," he interrupted. "I'm not sure I'd call her that."

"I want you to know, you don't need that gun," I stammered.

"She wanted to go to Applebaum's," he went on, as though he hadn't heard me, "and expected me to pay. I told her I was low on cash, but did she believe me? Nope, she did not." Then he broke out of thinking mode. "Hey, you start driving and quit talking."

"Do you know where Rashawna is?" I asked anyway.

"In the trunk."

As if on cue we heard several loud thunks coming from the rear of the car. I could tell that Rashawna hadn't suffered any disabling injuries by the furious noise that erupted from the trunk. I sat perfectly still so as not to upset the man with a gun pointed at my temple.

"Exactly where would you like to go?" I asked. Another thunk from the trunk along with a few muffled words.

"... innie! ... un is ... astic!"

I strained to hear. She thunked again, and Joel slammed his fist down on the seat. With lightning-like brilliance it dawned on me what she was saying, and I relaxed.

"Joel," I said in my most comforting voice, "do you really want to hurt us?"

"Shut up!" He pounded the seat again. "Both of you. Now drive, old lady."

"You got the wrong chapel back there in the mall," I said, "but your intention was good. Telling what you know or suspect about a crime is always good."

"That was you behind that screen?" He sounded surprised and a little less scary. I wondered how long he could keep up the tough guy act.

"Why don't you tell me what you had in mind when you told me you think you know who this shoelace killer is?"

"All I want you to do is drive." He wiggled the gun next to my ear, causing my silver hoop earring to swing. *Nobody* touches my earrings.

"I don't think I can do that, Joel." I still had half of the Taffy Tail in my hand. I whipped around and shoved it into the gun barrel. Plastic. That's what Rashawna was trying to tell me. The gun was plastic.

"Hey!" Joel grabbed the stump of Taffy Tail out and pulled the trigger, click, click, what a sorry little sound.

I pulled the lever beside the driver's seat and quickly popped the trunk from inside the car. I heard Rashawna thrashing to free herself. Then she leaped out and charged. She tore open the passenger side door, grabbed Joel by the collar and began to shake. His head whipped back and forth like one of those little bobble-head dolls, a Tonto one.

"Rashawna!" I heaved myself out of the driver's side and got behind her, trying to find a place to grab her skintight little skirt. Not so easy. I finally resorted to giving her a sharp whack across the arse end. She let go of Joel and turned on me, eyes blazing. Never underestimate the wrath of a woman who's been thrown into a trunk.

"Calm down," I said quietly, remembering my favorite proverb: a soft answer turns away wrath.

"He shoved me in your trunk!" she screeched. She looked the car over. "Don't you ever lock this thing?"

"You two settle down. Now what's this all about?" I used my full-throated assistant librarian voice.

Joel had crumpled back into the seat and was examining the Taffy Tail with exaggerated care, every trace of bravado gone. The plastic gun lay beside him on the seat.

"Look, get into the car, Rashawna," I ordered. My stomach growled. "I'm taking you both to supper, and we're going to get to the bottom of this."

"Okay, but I am not sitting next to him." Rashawna shot around to the passenger side and got in. She stared straight ahead, arms over chest, as we drove off.

I headed for my favorite hole in the wall fish fry, Mack's Pier, and we sat at a small, square table where a few cold fries lingered near the napkin holder. I covered them with a clean napkin, swooped the mess into a nearby trash container and sat down. A waitress bustled over and took our order, then hurried back to the kitchen.

"Humph," said Rashawna, wriggling into her seat. "Not exactly Applebaum's."

"No," I said very, very patiently, "but I'm paying."

"Sounds good to me," said Joel, glancing around the room. "Funky place."

"I'm not very hungry," growled Rashawna. She sniffed her hands. "That trunk could use some of that deodorant soap."

I chuckled. "My trunk is no spa, that's for sure. I might give the peach bar a try."

I was very relieved when the food arrived a few minutes later, and all was quiet as we concentrated on our crispy white fish sandwiches and vinegar fries. I have always believed that food, especially fried food, has the power to soothe jangled nerves. Rashawna, ever conscious of adding a single ounce to her size two figure, picked lightly at her plate, but she was calm. Hooray for that.

"Joel, what do you know about this situation?" I asked, wiping my fingers on a paper napkin. There were only two other people in the place, and I was mindful of the fry cook and waitress in the kitchen. It was behind the order counter a few feet to the rear and the left of us. I leaned slightly toward Joel. "Come on, spill."

He put his elbows on the table and leaned right back at me. "There's this guy who comes in to the Dollar Store and buys all the red shoelaces, the ones on the cardboard clown shoes right by the register."

"I saw them," I said, warming to the subject and him. "The girl behind the counter says the store sells a lot of them."

"That was from a new shipment of party stuff that came in yesterday. We've had to restock the shoelaces twice this month. And the girl must have been Selena," said Joel. "I was supposed to work this afternoon, but I was too scared." He looked over his shoulder as if the killer would pounce as he spoke. "Anyway, I didn't think much of it until I saw a short story about The Red Shoelace Killer on television. It was about that girl who got killed a couple of years ago; her mom just died. Well, my mind was working on the red shoelace thing, and then I started seeing this shoelace-buying guy around the mall, you know, like every day. It creeped me out."

"You creeped me out when you threw me in the trunk." Rashawna bristled and pushed her plate away, crossing her arms over her chest. She wasn't picking up on Joel's anxiety at all.

"I didn't want to do that," said Joel, pleading in his voice, "but you came storming along and started yelling at me. They could have heard you in China. People were looking."

"Well, you stood me up."

"I was so nervous when I went into the chapel, or what I thought was the chapel," Joel said, "that I didn't even recognize you when you came screaming into that room." Now the eyes were pleading as well. "You look so hot today."

"I do not recall that I screamed into any room," said Rashawna, her wounded dignity in full view. "Anyway, that's not the Lutheran chapel, that's where we work. It's Chapel Marketing." She jerked her chin at Joel.

"It sounded like screaming to me. Anyway, I got out of there fast." Joel turned to me. "Lady, I just took off for the parking lot. I had no clue it was your car."

"Call me Minnie," I said, "and it might be a stroke of fortune that you picked my car. So why *did* you throw Rashawna into the trunk?"

"I'll get to that," he said, glancing her way again. "That guy, the one who buys the laces? I think he knows I'm onto him. Yesterday he sat on one of the mall benches by the Dollar Store and stared at me for two hours. Two hours! Every time I passed the store entrance, he was there, staring." He shivered and whipped his head around when the front door opened. A woman and two small children came in and took a table across the room from us. Little kid chatter now filled Mack's Pier.

"So he's the reason you didn't go to work today," I said, glad for the noise to cover our conversation.

"You got that right."

"Would you be able to identify this guy if you saw him again?" I asked.

"Oh, yeah. When somebody stares holes through you for two days, you remember what he looks like."

"And the toy gun?"

"I grabbed it outta the kids' section at the store. I found one that I thought looked real, you know, just in case he did something."

"You thought a toy gun would fool him?" Rashawna snorted.

"Well, it fooled Minnie here," Joel said, tossing his thumb at me. "And in the parking lot where you caught up with me? The reason I shoved you in the trunk? He was following me."

Rashawna and I stared at Joel, mouths open.

"What?" Now it was Rashawna's turn to look around.

"Once I got Curly here safely inside the trunk, I jumped in the back seat of your car and slid down," said Joel. "He was only a few rows back, and I could see him turning slowly, looking for me, like in one of those old movies you watch when you're all alone at night. I was so scared when the car door opened. I almost passed out with relief when I saw it was you, Minnie, and not some guy with a handful of red shoelaces."

"You had a funny way of showing it," I shot back.

"Yeah, well, I'm sorry about that, but all I wanted to do was get away. I figured we'd get out of there, and I'd apologize later."

"So why didn't you go to the police or something?" asked Rashawna.

"I'm not on the best side of the law right now," said Joel. "I thought if I confessed to a minister, they could tell the cops."

"Oh great, just great," said Rashawna. "I'm dating a criminal."

"I'm not a criminal, just owing on a few traffic tickets."

"How many is a few?" I asked.

"Not sure, maybe twenty." Joel looked completely miserable and scared, but now that I had the whole story, I was even more anxious to get to my friend Detective Horowitz. It was late, but I thought it was important to get the information into competent hands as quickly as possible.

"Joel, I think Rashawna and I understand why you did what you did." I felt her glare. "I have a friend down at the police station, and I think we should tell him about this."

"I don't know about that. That might really set this guy off," said Joel.

"How's he gonna know?" asked Rashawna. "He's probably back in the parking lot, still looking for your sorry self."

Rashawna was beginning to grate on my nerves. I decided to take her back to her car at the mall and then persuade Joel to go to the police station with me. We'd let the parking ticket problem alone for now.

"Look, you don't know me hardly at all," Joel said, "but I've got a sense about people, you know?"

"Yeah, you *sense* they like to get thrown in trunks."

I'd had enough. We had to get rid of her. I stood up and grabbed my trash. "We're dropping you back at your car, Rashawna." I directed my most persuasive gaze at Joel. "Then I think you and I should take a trip to the police station."

"Fine with me." Rashawna pushed away from the table, stood up and dumped her almost full plate into the trashcan. I paid at the counter, and Joel and I followed her out the door, walking towards my car.

"This Horowitz guy, is he cool?" Joel began to get nervous again.

"I've known him for many years," I said. "He's as cool as they come, and since traffic court handles parking tickets, I won't mention them if you don't. Deal?"

"Deal," said Joel. "Yeah, I'm cool with that."

Three

"I've changed my mind," said Rashawna, settling herself this time beside Joel in the back seat. "I want to go with you guys."

"I noticed how you moved closer to me for protection back there when the door at the fish fry opened," said Joel.

"Well, you are a piece of work, aren't you?" she retorted. "You let Minnie pay for dinner, and then you think you're the big man."

"Why do you want to go with us, Rashawna?" I asked quickly, hoping to prevent another heated exchange. I pulled out of the parking lot and headed in the direction of the police station. We'd have to pass the mall to get there, so I could still drop her at her car if she changed her mind yet again.

"Okay, I'm still pretty mad at you, Joel, but I don't want to miss anything, either," she said. "This is more exciting than going home to the laundry." She sighed softly.

"Look," I said, "detective Horowitz is an old school friend of mine. I think he'll be willing — no, I know he'll be *eager* — to hear our story, but you two have to stop the bickering."

Silence from the back seat.

"Joel," I said, "you have to organize your thoughts. Think of why this guy frightens you. Detective Horowitz will want to know what he looks like and if he said anything to you. Did he make threatening moves, you know, things like that." It was completely dark by now, and I hoped the detective was still at the station. "The guy in the mall may have stared you down for two days, but I don't think giving someone the creeps is against the law. So anything else you have will be good."

It was so quiet in the back seat my curiosity got the better of me, and I shot a swift glance into the rear view mirror. It looked like Joel was swallowing Rashawna's face. So much for bickering.

"Rashawna," I hissed, "pay attention!" A little gasp escaped from her as she pulled away from Joel and sat up. "I want you to act like a lady," I said. "The last thing we need is for anyone to doubt our story, which is a little sketchy right now. You can't go all hysterical on us."

"Yeah," Joel purred. "I don't want to have to kiss you quiet again."

"Lady is my middle name," Rashawna said, giggling.

Why did I think their relationship was going to be like a Kentucky Rumbler roller coaster ride? I sighed and gave my full attention to the road. We cruised past the mall and made a right onto Troy-Schenectady Road. Five minutes later I pulled into the police station lot and parked. Now that we were here, little butterflies began kicking up a ruckus in my stomach, not so good after eating a big plate of crispy fish and vinegar fries. I stifled an unladylike belch.

"How come I'm so nervous all of a sudden?" asked Joel.

"Maybe it's because you've got iron pedal foot or something," said Rashawna.

"Rashawna," I said, my voice full of warning.

"I'm just teasing him, Min," she said, simpering. "I know he's a stand-up guy with just a little, uh, ticket problem."

"Never mind that," I said. "Do you know what you're going to tell the detective, Joel?"

"Yeah, yeah, let's just get this over with," he said as the back car door whooshed open.

I led the way as we pushed through the double front doors and approached the sergeant at the desk, Sam Hobart, according to his nametag. He looked us over and then grinned broadly. "What can I do for you folks tonight?" His gaze rested on Joel for a few seconds, and his brow crinkled. "Say, you look familiar to me except for that bandana thing."

"I guess I have one of those familiar faces," said Joel. He did one of those neck rolls baseball players do sometimes and turned slightly to avoid being over-scrutinized.

"Why would you be familiar to *him*, though?" said Rashawna, her jaw clenched.

"Lady — be a lady," I growled back at her.

"Miss?" said the sergeant, still grinning, "This happens all the time, probably my mistake. Now," he continued, looking at me, "what can I do for you?"

"We're here to speak with detective Horowitz," I said. "I hope he's in."

"You missed him by about ten minutes," said the sergeant. "Can I help, or do you want to leave a message for him?"

"Is he gone for the night, or may we wait for him?" I asked. I could feel Rashawna bristling and wanting to comment further on Joel's familiar face. I shot her a laser-sharp warning glance that she ignored.

"I'm afraid he's gone for the evening. Do you want to leave a message?" Hobart repeated.

"We're working on a hunch, Sergeant," I said. "It's just a few interesting bits about one of your older cases mentioned in the paper the other day," I added, "but it's not urgent ..."

"Yet," said Joel, finishing for me.

"Let me just leave my name and number. Tell Detective Horowitz I'll call him tomorrow." I wrote the information on the clipboard Sergeant Hobart handed to me and then signaled for Joel and Rashawna to follow me out.

I was just about whacked. "We'll head back to the mall, and you can pick up your car, Rashawna. Joel, do you need a ride somewhere?"

"I can catch a bus over by the Sears unless the swimsuit model here wants to drop me off home," he answered.

"I suppose I could," said Rashawna. "Wanna ride in the trunk?"

"Aw, I explained why ..."

"Get in the car," I said wearily. "You've got about ten minutes to figure out what to do. By the time we get back to the mall, I want it settled."

Rashawna got into the car first and let out an atomic shriek. "Don't you ever lock this thing?"

I opened the driver's side door and looked in. A red shoelace, tied in a triple bow, dangled from my rearview mirror.

In my best murder-solving fantasies, starring myself, I always balance action and presence of mind with grace and aplomb. But grace and aplomb, those floozies, took off for the tall grass in this very real situation. I glanced around for lurking figures, trying to steady the earthquake-like movements of my body. This evidence on my mirror of a real, live, crazed killer was too close for comfort — way, way too close. The guy could be anywhere. Had we been followed from the fish fry?

"Get that thing off the mirror," Rashawna demanded, pointing to the shoelace.

I pushed my head past the steering wheel and peered at the dangling red lace. It was the killer's token, all right, left at the crime scene, which I hoped my poor little Toyota wouldn't soon become.

"Want me to get it, Min?" asked Joel. He placed his hand on my shoulder, which was a surprising comfort.

I took a deep breath. "Nope, I've got it." I fished around in my handbag for a pencil or pen. The shoelace was evidence, and I didn't want to fool with it. I flipped it off the mirror and wrapped it in a clean tissue.

"You two stay here and look lively," I ordered. Joel tried hard not to look nervous. Rashawna had been rendered speechless by the very idea of a killer stalking us. "I'll take this back into the station," I said.

"Ohhhh no," said Rashawna. "I am goin' with you. Joel can be lookout."

"I've been creeped out and stalked for two days now, and I'm not going to be any lookout for some whack job killer," Joel retorted.

In the middle of our mutual fear assessments, a police car, lights flashing, no siren, pulled up in front of the

station. Two officers popped out like uniformed jack-in-
the-boxes, and one yanked open the back door of the
squad car. He grabbed the arm of the person inside and
motioned for her to get out.

"What the?" said Joel, turning towards the noise.

Rashawna and I followed his gaze. The woman turned
briefly to face us, and some little ding of recognition went
off in my head.

"We are outta here now," Joel ordered. "Get in the car.
Come on, come on."

"What is the matter with you?' Rashawna demanded.

Then I had it. The girl behind the counter at the Dollar
Store, that's who she was. Joel's panicked look made me
more than curious, but I picked up on his instinct to be
away from there pronto like Tonto. I pulled open the door
on the driver's side and got in. Joel got into the back.

"You can't leave me here!" Rashawna raced to the
other side of the car.

"Get in!" Joel and I said together.

I pulled away from the station, trying to be invisible
while I did it. The officers and the woman were heading
up the stairs and didn't seem to notice us. There were no
backward glances at us, no recognition of Joel by the girl.
Once on the road back to the mall, we all relaxed a little.

"Okay, Joel," I said. "What was that all about?"

"Yeah, we'd sure like to know," said Rashawna.

"That chick is pure evil, and I didn't want to be in the
station with her in there," said Joel. "I didn't tell you
before, but I think she and that shoelace guy know each
other. I don't know why they hauled her in just now, but
I'll bet it's got something to do with him."

"She didn't exactly seem like pure evil when I spoke with her in the store this afternoon," I said. "Well, maybe a little irritated at you, was all."

"Yeah, and she would have let me have it with a string of cussing that would peel the paint off the station walls, and you should see some of the places she's pierced," said Joel. "Her tats would make your skin crawl."

Yikes, Joel was laying it on pretty thick, and Rashawna was all ears, too.

"Tats?" I ventured.

"Tattoos," said Rashawna as she turned to Joel. "There must be a reason why you know this stuff about her."

"Let's just get away from here. I'll tell you about it sometime," he said.

"Yeah, I'll bet that will be real interesting." Rashawna raised an eyebrow at me in the rear view mirror and abruptly changed the subject. "I wish I'd just gone back to my own car," she wailed. "I don't think I can take this kind of excitement. I don't want to know about anybody doing anything anywhere."

"Hey," said Joel gently, "it's okay. Since we've only been together for three days, almost nobody knows anything about you or even knows that you know me, right, Min?"

"That's right," I said, blanching just a little at the assigned nickname. "By the time the shoelace guy was near Joel at the mall, you were already out of sight."

"And you know why, Honey?" purred Joel. "Because I had the good sense to throw you in the trunk."

Oh, boy. I didn't want to get started on that again. "Almost to your car," I said, making my voice upbeat. "Rashawna, do you have somewhere you'd rather stay tonight instead of home alone, maybe with a relative or something?"

"Uh, why would I have to do that, Minnie? You two are just done telling me I'm outta danger."

"You are, Babe," said Joel, taking more liberties with the terms of endearment. "It's just that we're being careful."

"I don't know," she said, softening.

It had been a long, weird evening, and Rashawna was confused, upset and agitated, not unlike Joel and me.

"You could stay with me," I offered. "I have one of those sofa-chair thingies that makes into a single bed."

"Could we run by my place so I can get a change of clothes and my toothbrush?" Rashawna asked.

"Sure thing," I answered. "When we get to your car, I'll follow you home." We pulled up alongside her car a few minutes later. Joel opened my car door and hopped out. He looked around, trying very hard to appear cool and pulled together. I had a feeling, though, that if an empty shopping bag blew by he'd jump like a flea on a hot sidewalk.

"All clear," he said. The parking lot was still pretty crowded. A new bistro had opened in the mall, and the owners were trying to get a jump on business by offering Monday night specials.

"Go on," I said as Rashawna got out of my car and scurried to hers. "I'll follow you."

"Wait!" said Joel. He dashed after her, opened the driver's side door of her car and peered inside. He opened the back door and felt under the front seats. This gesture of caution and concern had an amazing effect on Rashawna. When he pulled himself back from his inspection of the car's interior, she threw her arms around his neck and planted one on his lips.

"Oh, yeah," he said, grabbing her around the waist and pulling her against him.

"Thank you so much, but I gotta go," she purred, backing away. Rashawna ducked into the driver's seat, turned the motor over and began to back out.

I watched as Joel sauntered off into a crowd of bistro-bound, noisy teenagers.

Four

To say that Rashawna was driving cautiously would be an understatement of titanic proportions. She was going so slow she actually made me nervous. Through her rear window I saw her dark curls slapping her cheeks as she swung her head first to one side, then the other, while she monitored the cars around her. What was she thinking, that the killer would pop up alongside her on the Harley from Hell and death ray her while she drove? Maybe. I just hoped it wasn't too much farther to her home. I had no idea where she lived. Our age difference kept us from being real gal pals, so we hadn't shared too many personal details of our lives; but we worked together three days a week and every other weekend. We had a friendly co-worker's knowledge of each other.

Rashawna swerved and stopped suddenly right in front of me, her car mostly off the shoulder with her rear bumper presented to oncoming traffic. I nearly stood my car on end when I came up behind her. She whipped the car door open, leaped out and ran toward me.

I rolled my window down and called to her. "What on earth are you doing? You can't jump out of your car in the middle of the road like this!" I immediately put on my emergency flashers.

I felt a whoosh of air as my passenger door swung open.

"I know he's watchin' us, Minnie, I just know it." Her hands were flapping like hummingbird wings.

"Well, he's going to watch your car get smashed to bits if you don't get it out of the road," I said. I backed my car up and pulled onto the shoulder. "Give me your keys."

"Just pull it over there," she said. "The cops won't bother it for a whole day."

"I'm sure there's a really good reason why you know that." I didn't have time to hear her response, because traffic was coming up behind us fast. I got out of my car and dashed to hers. An SUV sped by, the driver honking and offering finger gestures, just as I got her ancient Nissan pulled over and locked up. I hurried back to my car.

"Oh, thank you, Minnie," Rashawna gasped. "I guess I just had a little panic attack. My place is only three miles or so from here." She sank back on the seat and held a hand over her heart. "Go to the next light and turn left."

"I hope you know what you're doing," I said, easing my car back onto the road. I turned at the light, and we went on for four more blocks, turned again, and then she directed me to a short dirt and gravel road at the end of which sat a white, Cape Cod-style house. "Oh," I said, "this is lovely."

"I get a good deal on the rent, but you see how dark it is back here? I just didn't want to pull into the road all alone, even with you behind me." She peered into the little copse of woods sheltering one side of the driveway and shivered.

"Well, I don't blame you for that," I said. I will not think of the murderer, I will not think of the murderer.

"I ran out of here so fast this morning, I forgot to turn on a light."

"Open the glove box," I said. "I have a flashlight in there."

"Suppose there's a shoelace in there?"

"Oh, for heaven's sake," I said, reaching across her to pop the box open. I took out my small, red emergency flashlight and checked to make sure it still worked. "Come on."

Rashawna unlocked the front door, pushed it open and turned on the hall light. We did a hip-to-hip search of the house, and no skulking killer seemed to be about. Rashawna walked down a hallway and disappeared into a back bedroom. When she returned, I saw she'd grabbed pants and a shirt, makeup bag and underclothes, and had retrieved a grocery bag from somewhere in the kitchen into which she was stuffing everything. She made sure to leave lights on this time, one under the cupboard in the kitchen and the one on the post in the yard. She locked the front door, and we returned to my car. The light from the post cast a circle of light that reached a little way into the road in front of Rashawna's house. Was that a car sitting there just beyond the edge of the light? I didn't want to set Rashawna off again, so I didn't mention it, but I didn't waste any time getting out of there, either.

I kept my eye in the rear view mirror and didn't see anyone following us, so I relaxed a little, chalking it up to my overstimulated imagination. My own apartment was in Rensselaer, and we had to get on the bridge to cross the Hudson River to get there. Once over the bridge we pulled onto I-90 and headed east. Boy, was I ever tired now. I hoped Rashawna didn't mind sleeping on that chair bed thingy, because the spare bedroom was packed to the ceiling with the accumulated junk of a lifetime. My husband had been gone for ten years, but I'd only recently managed to whittle our belongings down from two storage rental units to that one overstuffed spare room.

It was almost nine o'clock when I opened my front door. I threw my bag of Taffy Tails onto the kitchen table and showed Rashawna where to put her things. "Would you like a cup of tea?" I asked.

"Oh, Minnie, I love tea."

Well, what a nice surprise. It was good to know we had one thing in common. I set the teakettle on a burner and turned on the television while Rashawna used the bathroom. I grabbed a Taffy Tail and collapsed into my recliner. I'd watched six commercials and was done with my treat by the time the teakettle blew. I went back to the stove, measured some Earl Grey into a tea ball and poured the hot water into my Rockingham teapot. I set it on the counter to steep and heard Rashawna coming out of the bathroom.

"Minnie, that soap in there is divine," she said to my back as I opened the cupboard to get out two mugs. "Where did you get it?"

"It's goat's milk soap. I buy it at a little farmers' market down in Kinderhook," I answered. "They're open every Saturday in the summer."

I found what I was looking for, two big red mugs I'd gotten on sale at Macy's the previous Christmas, perfect wrap-your-hands-around mugs. I turned to show them to Rashawna and nearly sent them crashing to the floor at the sight of her. She had her curls twirled up in white rags, her cheeks were shiny with face cream, and she wore the skimpiest nightie I'd ever seen. She touched her hair when she saw my face.

"Um, I'll bet you don't see this every day, do you?"

"Well, no … no, I don't," I said, recovering a little. "What happened to the rest of that nightie?"

She laughed. "You think this is skimpy? You should have seen some of the swimsuits I had to model." She twirled so her rag curls bounced, and she winked at me. "It's softer to sleep on my hair this way." I was relieved to see that she was regaining some of her confidence and energy.

"Let's have this tea," I said, pouring a steaming cup for each of us.

"This is kind of fun," Rashawna said as she grabbed the big cup handle.

I picked up my mug, and we sat down. The volume on the television was low, but I turned it up when I saw the face on the news.

"Hey," said Rashawna, "that looks like …"

"The woman we saw at the police station," I finished the sentence for her.

"… arrested on charges of aggravated assault," said the reporter.

"Min, what do you suppose she did? What about the guy Joel saw? Do you think … ?"

"… in a domestic dispute," the reporter continued.

"I don't know what to think, Rashawna," I said, my eyes intent on the television.

"She does look evil, just like Joel said." Rashawna squinted at the screen. "Look at those eyes."

I raised an eyebrow. We couldn't really see her eyes. Some reporter must have gotten wind of the arrest and turned up after Joel, Rashawna and I left the police station. The biggest newspaper in the city had its offices only a mile or two up the road from there, after all.

"Well, if Joel says she's evil, I'll bet she is. Good tea." Rashawna continued to watch the television screen and took another sip. "What's a domestic dispute?"

"Violence in the home," I answered.

"Oh, yeah, I knew that," she said, "like she was busting on her old man."

"Rashawna, may I ask you something?"

"Sure, Minnie, shoot," she said. She snuggled into the chair and smiled.

"How or where did you meet Joel?"

Her eyes glazed over, all dreamy. "Oh, Minnie, it was so romantic. He ran his hand up my leg."

"*What?*"

She waved her free hand back and forth. "Wait, wait. That wasn't a very good way to say it." She cleared her throat, giggled and took another sip of tea. "Have you got anything sweet?"

"Sure, hang on," I said, getting out of my chair. I took a Taffy Tail out of the bag and handed it to her. She tore the wrapper down and took a bite. "Mmm, this is really good."

"So?" I said.

"Oh, yeah," said Rashawna, her voice a little muffled from the chewy candy in her teeth. "I had to run to the Dollar Store last Friday for some shampoo, and while I was on tiptoe, looking for my brand on the top shelf, this rotten little kid sneaked up behind me with a can of shaving cream." She took another, rather vicious, bite of the Taffy Tail. "Humph," she said, remembering the little scamp. "Anyway, he shot it up my skirt just as Joel came around the corner. I was so embarrassed. Joel had paper towels and some window cleaner in his hands, and he used the towels to scrape the stuff off my legs."

"Gosh, you two are a regular Meg Ryan and Billy Crystal," I said.

"Who?"

"From the movie, *When Harry Met Sally*?"

"Must be a really old one, never heard of it," she said. "Never mind," I said, "I'm surprised Joel didn't chase the little trouble maker."

"Oh, he yelled at him, and the kid ran for cover," she said. "You wonder where the Mom is sometimes, don't you." She looked thoughtful as she finished her tea and candy. "So then, when he asked me out, what could I say?"

"There have been stranger first meetings, I'm sure," I said. I stood up and indicated the blue chair that would soon be transformed into her bed for the night. "Let me show you how to unfold this chair."

Suddenly the news program had our attention again. "Joel Rodriguez called in the complaint," the reporter said, wrapping up his report.

Rashawna and I turned as if we were one person to stare at the television screen.

"Oh, Minnie," she said, panic in her eyes. "It can't be, can it?"

"I don't even know what to say," I stammered, "but wait a minute. Do you actually know Joel's last name?"

"Well, no."

"This could be just a coincidence," I said.

"Well, a pretty darn weird one, if you ask me. Maybe Joel really does know why that chick is evil. Maybe she visited it on him once or twice."

I puffed out my cheeks and stared at her. Visited it on him? Unbelievable. "When are you going to see him again?"

"I don't know," she said, throwing up her hands. "I know there's gotta be more than one Joel in the world, but this is too, uh ..."

"Unsettling," I said, finishing her thought. I knew Rashawna's very short relationship with Joel meant she probably knew next to nothing about him. I also guessed that an immediate physical attraction like they seemed to have, shaving cream and all, might overshadow little things like last names or marital status.

"But he was with us," said Rashawna. "Did you see him use his phone?"

"No, but he could have done that right after he left the mall and before the trunk incident. Still, he didn't seem hurt when we were with him," I responded.

"Unless she clobbered him where the sun don't shine."

"That could be why he called her evil. For most guys where the sun don't shine is a very sensitive spot."

"Oh, my poor baby," whimpered Rashawna. "Maybe he's sleeping on a bench outside the Sears store right now."

The truth was, we just didn't know, but I had no more energy to give to the problem, and I couldn't see any reason why we had to worry about it right at that moment. My bed was calling me. "Well, he's somewhere off in the night, and we can't do much at this hour. Let's sleep on it,

Rashawna. I'll fix us a nice breakfast in the morning, and we can rehash everything that's happened."

"Okay, I guess I could try to sleep," she said, plopping down on the chair bed. She pulled the blue blanket over her knees and wrapped her arms around them. "Things always look different in the morning, don't they?"

"They do," I said, admiring this bit of wisdom from her.

"Do you have an extra pillow?" she asked. "I need one to hug, or I won't fall asleep."

"Sure, I have lots of them," I said. Then I had a blinding thought. "Your car," I blurted, remembering it on the side of the road. "I almost forgot about your car."

"No problem," she said, stifling a yawn. "The cops don't cruise by there until nine in the morning, and we can pick it up before then—plus, I spit-hexed it."

"Spit-hexed it?"

"Yeah, it's a little thing my Aunt Lucretia showed me." She put her index and middle fingers in her mouth, took them out and made an X in the air. "Just like that, right on the window, works every time, too. You have to remember to use these two fingers though," she said, holding the slightly damp digits out for me to examine.

I had a blurry vision of her pausing at the car window before she'd run to my car. "I don't even want to know," I said, stifling a yawn of my own. I retrieved a medium plump pillow from my spare room and tossed it to her.

"Thanks, Minnie," said Rashawna. "You're a good person."

I smiled and took myself off to my bedroom. I was hoping I wasn't too tired to sleep. Just before I conked out,

I heard Rashawna snoring lightly. So much for her not being able to sleep.

Five

Somewhere in the middle of my superb dream about a vacation in Paris with a handsome, gray-templed gentleman named Gregor, I sensed a wild thumping sound coming from what seemed like a great distance.

"Minnie, we're late! Wake up!"

I rolled over and looked at the alarm clock, which had apparently gone off without my noticing. It was 8:40 a.m. Oh, great. It took every ounce of early morning effort I had to pull myself away from Gregor, the Brie and Bordeaux, but when I did, the whole bed shook.

"Oh, no! We're due at the mall in twenty minutes."

"I know," shrieked Rashawna, "and my car! Hurry up!"

I yanked the bedroom door open and bolted into the bathroom. Rashawna was already there, pulling the rags out of her hair and fighting me for the sink.

"Only time for a chorus girl's bath," I squawked as I dashed warm water into my armpits and smeared on deodorant.

"Chorus girls got nothin' on us," Rashawna chimed in, fingering her curls as she sloshed toothpaste onto the toothbrush balancing on the edge of the sink.

With a comic routine of chaotic ducking and dodging, we both managed to be presentable in about eight minutes. Forget breakfast. We did a Three Stooges door jam on our way out of the bathroom, my bulk just barely beating her back.

"Ooooh, I hope that cop got stuck behind some fat chick making tough choices at the Krispy Kreme," said Rashawna, slipping on her shoes and grabbing her handbag.

"I think we're good, we'll make it," I said, not meaning it at all. What Rashawna really didn't need right now was an illegal parking ticket. "I sure wish I believed in hexes." That stopped her cold.

"That's right," said Rashawna, snapping her fingers. "I almost forgot about my spit-hex. For sure that cop will be late today."

"Just like we're going to be late if we don't get a move on," I said, looking at my watch. We had just enough time to stop for her car and hightail it to the mall. Our supervisor at Chapel Marketing expected a call from the job site at nine sharp.

"Man, I'm starving," said Rashawna. She got into my car and whipped her seat belt over. She sighed heavily and clutched her midsection.

"We'll have to grab something from one of the mall food vendors," I said. The road was clear when I pulled out of the apartment complex parking lot, and I let my foot be a little heavy on the gas pedal. In a few minutes we approached the spot where we'd left Rashawna's Nissan. It was still there, looking forlorn and abandoned but unmolested, as far as we could tell. I had a weak moment and wondered what other things a double finger spit-hex might work on, like the extra pounds on my rear end, maybe. I dropped Rashawna off on the shoulder behind the vehicle, and she trotted over to it, keys jangling. She waved me on after eyeballing the inside of the car. I pulled out and sped up I-90.

I screeched into mall lot H and parked. It was 8:58. It took me exactly ninety seconds to reach the pay phone just outside the main mall entrance, and I dialed my supervisor's number and tried like crazy to breathe normally. Her assistant answered.

"Hi, Deidre," I wheezed, "Minnie here. Clock me in, will you?"

"You're in the parking lot, aren't you? I hear street noises," she said.

"Well, I can't put anything over on you, can I?" I put a chuckle into my voice. "Overslept by just a few," I said, knowing she'd let it go. "It's nine sharp, and I'm here. You know how many times I've stayed over to finish up a survey, don't you? And with no pay."

"Yup, I do, and we love you for it," Deidre said, chuckling back. "Don't worry about it, you're clocked in. Have a great one, Minnie." She rang off.

Ten minutes later Rashawna and I were in headsets and had resumed our survey taking positions, each with a steaming cup of coffee and a blueberry muffin in hand from Muffins at the Mall. We usually didn't get any takers in the early hours, so after I set up for the day's surveys, I relaxed with my hastily bought breakfast. I'd picked up a morning paper, too. There was no mention of the previous night's arrest on the front page, but a short blurb popped up a few pages in, in the police blotter. The 911 call had come in at 6:10 for the domestic violence situation. A woman matching the description of the Dollar Store clerk was reported, and the caller, her husband, was identified as Joe Rodriguez. Apparently, she'd thrown several glass bottomed … My eyes traveled back over the sentence. Joe, it read Joe, not Joel. Somebody had made a big boo-boo on the television report last night, and I was surprised to find myself greatly relieved.

"Rashawna," I said into my headset, "if there are no prospects out there right now, would you come back here for a minute?"

"Sure, Minnie," she mumbled through blueberry muffin.

"Look at this," I said. I handed her the newspaper as she came into the hole. She wiped her hands free of muffin crumbs and took the paper, quickly scanning the story.

"I see it, Minnie," she said, "Joe, the guy's name is Joe. What a relief."

"What's a relief?" a voice said behind us.

We turned to see Joel standing in the doorway. He had a different colored bandana covering his head this morning and a half-smile on his face.

"Oh, Honey!" Rashawna shrieked. She ran to him and threw her arms around his neck. "It wasn't you!"

"No, no it wasn't," he said, seeming not to care what he wasn't. Wrapping himself around her, he glanced at me and winked as he murmured through her apple-scented curls, the opportunist.

"You haven't got any clue what we're talking about have you?" I asked.

Rashawna pulled back and took his face in her hands. "That devil woman you work with, the one we saw last night? She made the evening news."

"No kidding," he said. "What did they have on her? I hope you two slept okay last night." He came farther inside and took a seat.

"So good we overslept," I said. "Joel, what's the story with your co-worker? The television report says she was picked up for domestic violence."

"Yeah, her poor husband Joe," said Joel. "He picked her up from work one day early last week, and he had a whopper of a black eye. I think she must beat him up good every once in a while just for the sport of it. She is evil."

"Well, we're glad it wasn't you," said Rashawna.

"You thought it was me?"

"The television report got the name wrong," I said. "They said Joel instead of Joe."

"Yeah, and since we don't know your last name, we just jumped to a conclusion," said Rashawna, only slightly abashed.

"You thought I ratted on Selena? You thought I was her husband?"

"Joel, we did rush to judgment, but really, can you blame us? Your reaction at the police station was pretty strong."

"And you never did tell me your last name," said Rashawna, "or about being a familiar face at the police station," she added.

"Okay, I guess you got me," said Joel. "First off, my last name is Fabio. Okay?"

Rashawna's brows and mine went up at the same time.

"Don't say it," Joel barked, "and I don't know a lot about Selena, either. We had lunch together once, and all she did was complain about the guy she's married to, Joe. And the name calling! Whoa, that chick has a serious attitude problem, a potty mouth, and a temper like the devil."

"Actually, I got a little taste of her temper when I was in the store yesterday and asked if they sold a lot of those red shoelaces," I said. "She really blew up when I asked about you."

"Yeah? I didn't know you asked about the shoelaces," said Joel.

"Who would buy them anyway, like who and why?" Rashawna asked, palms up. The tone of her voice screamed fashion police.

"I just thought of something," I said. "Suppose the guy you saw was watching Selena and not you, Joel? What if there's some connection to the killer there?"

"Why did he follow me to the parking lot, then?" Joel asked.

"That's a good question and one we don't know the answer to, but right now we have to get back to work," I said, glancing into the mall. The morning wore on, and the mall was filling up. We still had to get about twenty more deodorant soap surveys. A lot of the shoppers were prime targets, too, so I shooed Rashawna off to the escalator while Joel drifted toward the Dollar Store. Now that Selena was temporarily out of the picture, he would put in another day there.

The rest of the morning and the early afternoon passed without incident, and we were only short six surveys by four o'clock. The next hour, between four and five, was always tough. It was transition time in the mall, and getting people to take surveys was usually a lost cause.

Rashawna often sat on the bench near the end of the escalator, the one where husbands waited and suffered while their wives ripped apart sale racks and clattered through bargain shoes that were all in the wrong sizes and colors. As I sorted the stack of our finished surveys, I heard Rashawna's voice weakly in my headset.

"Minnie," she whispered, "something's not right."

"What?" I said, not quite catching it.

"I think it's him," she squeaked. "Okay, I'm getting up slowly and grinning like you just told me a joke, hanging onto my ear, you know. I'm coming back over there. Act natural."

I stood up and moved to the doorway as naturally as possible. Rashawna was putting on a pretty unnatural show. A couple of teenage boys eyeballed her as she sashayed toward me with her hand on her ear, inclining her head to the left.

"What on earth are you talking about?" I asked when she got near.

"Joel told me a little about that guy, the one who stared at him, remember?" Rashawna said as she threw her head back in a false laugh.

"I do. And?"

Putting her hand on my elbow Rashawna steered me away from the entrance to our space. "The same guy has passed on the other side of the benches about six times this afternoon," she said. "He looked me right in the eye just now. And something's wrong with his forehead. It's kind of weird."

"His forehead? Do you think you might be a little paranoid?" I asked, pulling back to look at her.

"Can I stay with you again tonight?" she asked, ignoring my question. "This is creeping me out so bad." No more false laugh. Her face was now a picture of woe.

We'd disappeared from the view of any shoppers. I calmed her with an arm around her shoulder and sat her in the chair across from me. "Now, let's start at the very beginning," I said. "What did Joel tell you?"

"About the guy?"

"About the guy."

"Uh, well, he's not very tall, he has dark messy hair and, oh, yeah, he's got really big feet." She shivered and looked out into the mall. "That's kind of a weird thing to notice, I know. Plus, he was all over the place in this mall today. I wonder if he sat outside the Dollar Store again."

"Are you pretty sure it's the same guy? How far across the mall was he from you?"

With furrowed brow Rashawna said, "I'm pretty sure. The height was right, and he had the glary thing going. He was maybe twenty feet from me. Yeah, twenty feet."

She seemed satisfied with her judge of distance. "Problem is, the mall is a public place, and if this guy didn't do anything threatening, there's nothing we can do right now," I said, putting my hands on both of her shoulders, getting her to focus. "Are you and Joel going out tonight?"

"Yeah, he gets paid today, and we're going to Applebaum's for sure tonight."

"Okay, here's what you do. Ask Joel if he noticed this fella staring at him from the bench again today," I instructed.

"Oh, poor Joel. The creep!" Then she caught herself. "Oh, not Joel, the guy."

"Yeah, I got that. Anyway, if Joel noticed him too, this will test my theory of whether the guy was staring at Joel or Selena for the past two days," I said.

"Oh, good thought, Minnie," said Rashawna. "It could have zip to do with Joel."

"That's right. Now, I want you and Joel to compare notes at dinner. Have him write down a description of the guy he saw. Tell him to be precise. He might be the same guy you saw — or not. I'll see if I can get in touch with Detective Horowitz again. Who knows what we'll find?"

"So is that a yes?"

"What?"

"About staying with you again tonight," she said. There was a little tremble in her voice.

I sighed. "We'll see. Call me when you and Joel are done with dinner."

I sent her back to the escalator, but I knew she wouldn't be her perky, friendly self for the few minutes we had left. Chapel Marketing gave us fifteen minutes of clearing up time, and I had to do an end-of-the-day call before we left to report our survey count for the day. As luck would have it, I got Deirdre again.

"Well, how'd it go today, Minnie? All done?" she asked, bursting with cheer.

"We need six more to complete the survey. I'm sure we can churn those out in the morning," I said.

"Oooh," said Deirdre, "boss lady won't like that. Corporate's been breathing down her neck. These puppies have to be in on time, or the client may drop us for future work."

"Tell you what," I said, "as soon as we finish the last six, I'll run them all over to the office. I should be there by ten."

"That'll have to do, I guess. There's a big meeting at ten-thirty, so the sooner, the better. Anyway, have a nice evening," Deirdre said and rang off.

Six

On my way out of the mall I grabbed a gyro and a diet soda at my favorite Greek fast food counter. I'd have to eat it in the car on my way to the police station. I was pretty sure I'd catch up to Dan before he left, as it was at least two hours earlier than when we'd been there the night before. I got into my car and took a few minutes to enjoy my quick supper. Gyros were something I'd discovered several years ago when the Roaring Gate Mall got a serious renovation. Since then, all kinds of new eating places had come to the food court. A lot had gone, too. But I loved these pita sandwiches stuffed with shaved, garlicky lamb and loaded with tomatoes, onions and cucumber yogurt sauce. It was the perfect car food, too, because it was all contained in a tidy paper wrapper. I took a few bites and started the car. I was done with the gyro and almost all of the soda by the time I turned the corner and saw the steps of the police station. I wondered — I hoped — one of the cars out front was Dan's. I grabbed one of those thin mouthwash strips that I kept in my purse to erase the evidence of onion-eating occasions and laid it on my tongue. I swiped a True Berry lipstick across my mouth, ran my fingers through my hair and got out of the car. I so wanted to pop the button at the top of my pants.

The station door opened just as I got to the bottom of the steps, and Dan Horowitz came through, escorting a gorgeous blonde. They were deep in conversation. I didn't know what to do, so I slowed down and stopped as they descended the steps toward me. Why was I feeling like such an idiot? Suddenly Dan threw his head back and laughed. He leaned over and kissed the woman on the cheek and waved to her as she continued on without him. Then he saw me.

"Minnie!" he boomed. "How nice to see you. The sergeant told me you'd stopped by last night. So sorry I missed you."

He held out his hand and noticed my eyes following the blonde.

"My niece, Edwina," he said. "She's studying forensics at SUNY, Albany, and we just finished up a short interview." He smiled at her quickly retreating form. "Her mother, my sister, is appalled at Edwina's choice of studies, but I think she'll do just fine. She's really into the autopsy part of her program right now, too." Dan turned back to me. "Have you eaten?"

"Yes, I have," I said, glad that the little breath strip had taken care of the telltale garlic and onion odor, "but if you're on your way to supper, I'll go with you and have my tea. There's a curious situation I'd like to talk to you about."

"Wonderful," he said. "There's a neat little fish fry I always go to on my late nights, Mack's Pier. They have some nice crispy white fish and great fries. It's not too far."

But their tea isn't so great, I thought. Oh, well, I wasn't going for the food at Mack's but only to get Dan's input about the strange happenings in the mall over the last few days. He walked me to his car, helped me in, and we pulled into Mack's about ten minutes later. The fry cook looked up as we walked in and got out his pad on his way over to take our order. It looked like he was chief cook, bottle washer and wait staff for the evening. I wondered if he'd caught the little scene that Joel, Rashawna and I had made the night before when we'd left his fine eatery.

"Back again, huh?" he said, looking at me and licking the tip of his stubby pencil.

"Just can't stay away," I answered lamely. So much for not being noticed. Dan only arched an eyebrow before he ordered his crispy white fish and vinegar fries. I ordered tea with extra lemon and an apple turnover.

"So, you like this place, too?" Dan asked.

"I'm a real fan of anything deep fried," I said. I'd known Dan for almost ten years, and I'd learned that he was kind, helpful and funny. He wasn't a very handsome man, but he made up for it with the sheer force of his personality. He was almost six feet tall, with thinning, rust-colored hair, gray eyes, and cheeks that were just beginning to jowl. I'd taken his criminal justice course at a local community college right after my husband died, and Dan and I were instantly attracted to each other's thought processes about crime, criminals and the whole justice system in general. He was several years younger than I and had a lovely wife, Leanne, and two daughters. I hoped he'd be willing to listen to my suspicions about the shoelace killer and not think I was wasting his time.

"C'mon Minnie, spill," said Dan. "Do you think you've found something out about the shoelace killer? I'll bet the paper caught your eye on that one." He winked at me.

Boy, no surprising this guy. He'd read me. "I'm not sure, but enough things have happened in the last few days that my radar is cranked up. I may be way off on it, but I don't think so." I told him about my first encounter with Joel, the incident with my car trunk and Selena, the mad Dollar Store clerk. I also told him about finding the red shoelace on my car's rear view mirror as we were about to leave the station the night before.

"So the three of you came down to see me last night."

"Actually, we'd just eaten here," I explained.

"Really? Does that seem significant?" he asked.

"It's possible we were followed here from the mall. If the man Joel saw was still in the parking lot, he may have seen the ruckus by the trunk."

"From the way you tell it, it was quite a scene," he said, grinning.

"Rashawna has a fiery temper when she's upset," I said. "It's very possible that the guy laid low and then followed us here, but he took a real chance putting the shoelace in my car while we were inside the station."

"Some of these guys just love it on the edge," said Dan. "I remember one guy, a purse snatcher, who couldn't resist grabbing at his victim's rear end just before he tore off down the street." Dan chuckled.

"I do hope you caught him."

"Sure did. The grabbing was his downfall. It slowed him down, and the young officer who took off after him was too fast for him."

"Was that young officer you?"

"Aw, how'd you guess?" Dan's eyes sparkled now.

I smiled back at him. "Anyway, I still don't see why this guy would be bothering us."

"There's probably a connection you just haven't made yet. You've only been putting your excellent mind to the problem for a short time."

I blinked and then blushed. "Like I said, my radar is cranked up."

Dan looked around the room, and his eyes settled on the cook, busily preparing our order. "Do you suppose he saw anything? He seemed to recognize you just now when we ordered. It's pretty tight quarters in here, and the big window looks right out on the street."

I followed Dan's eyes. The window needed a good washing, but the whole street and a distance up some of the side streets were clearly visible through it. "Huh," I said, "couldn't hurt to ask him. My excellent mind didn't veer off in that direction, I guess."

"He looks like he gets right at his cooking, with not a lot of his attention going to the tables," said Dan, "but you're right, it couldn't hurt to ask."

Moments later the cook set our piping hot food in front of us. I was about to ask the man if he'd seen anything, when the door opened and six rowdy, hungry-looking teens exploded into the dining area. The cook left us and greeted them, pulling out his order pad as he spoke.

"It's okay," said Dan, watching the little scene, "we can ask him later. Let's enjoy this." He tackled his fish and vinegar fries with obvious relish, adding extra malt vinegar to the food from a bottle on the table. I noticed, not for the first time, that Dan was one of those people who seemed to be able to eat anything and not gain an ounce. It was about the only thing I didn't like about him. I dipped my tea bag up and down a few times and tried to figure out which end of my apple turnover to tackle first. The cook had warmed it, for which I silently thanked him.

I inclined one ear to the table of teens, and one of them addressed the cook as Eddie and placed a double order of fish and fries for the whole gang. Eddie left their table and returned in a few minutes with drinks before heading back to the kitchen to fry up their order. The noise level in the room went up considerably as the group talked and joked with each other.

"Busy place tonight," I said. Dan smiled as he popped a final vinegar fry into his mouth. My apple turnover was a bit dry, and I was glad I had the hot tea to wash it down.

"I don't think I can hang around and wait to question the cook," said Dan. "My case load has been brutal lately. Is there another time that you could come back and talk to him?" He nodded in the direction of the kitchen.

"Oh, I'm sure I can get around to it in a day or so," I said.

"You know, I'm only seeking information," Dan said cautiously. "We'll always welcome input from observant citizens, and it can sometimes be helpful, but we have people on this case."

"Oh, don't I know it," I said. "I fully realize I have no authority at all, but I also guess that you're all stretched pretty thin."

"Well, I won't argue that. So you understand, then?"

"I do," I said, "and I had another thought."

"Okay, shoot."

"Is there any way I could talk to Selena? Joel and I have our suspicions about her."

"Sure, if you can find her," said Dan. "She only spent the night in the holding cell. Her husband came in this morning and said he didn't want to press charges."

"I wonder if he could be the one Rashawna saw in the mall today," I said, thinking Selena may be the sort to step out on her husband, and the resulting blowup had gotten him a black eye. It must have been quite a bruiser, too, for Joel to notice it the one time he'd seen the man. Was Selena's husband prowling the mall, looking for his wife's lover? Or maybe Selena and her husband were a couple of psychotics using the mall as a base — or something. Anyway, it was worth a shot if I could get up my nerve to face the evil Selena again. Dan interrupted my thoughts and stood up.

"I'll get this, Minnie," he said, pulling some bills from his wallet and walking to the counter. Eddie popped his head up from among the spitting fryers and motioned for Dan to leave the money under a coffee mug on the counter near the cash register. Did I mention this was a hole-in-the-wall place? Coffee mug cash-out says it all.

"I hope you don't mind my curiosity about this case," I said as we stepped towards the door. "But it almost seems I'm being dragged into it whether I like it or not, with the shoelace on the car mirror and all. It's frightening and exciting at the same time."

Dan tossed his head and laughed. "That's what I love about you, Minnie. You say what you think, and it's almost exactly what I think. By the way, do you still have the shoelace?"

"I do," I said, suddenly excited to be able to give him some hard evidence of what I'd been telling him. I pawed through my handbag and pulled it out. The tissue I'd wrapped it in had one lipstick blot on it, which I pointed out to Dan. He took it and carefully placed it in his jacket pocket.

"Fresh out of little bags," he said, winking, "but thanks for this. I'll get it to the lab and let you know if it has any trace on it. To answer your other concern, I don't mind your curiosity at all. One thing, though," he said, looking rather stern.

"What's that?"

"If you perceive any real danger, call the station," he said. "Don't let the excitement get the better of you."

"No problem there," I said.

"All right, that's good."

Dan drove me back to my car, and I told him I'd stay in touch.

It was quite dark by the time I was back in my own car, and as I drove past the mall I knew the Dollar Store would still be open. I had no idea if Selena was back working the evening shift, and I decided to head home. I needed to formulate my thoughts and figure out what I wanted to find out from her anyway, so I didn't feel bad about letting it go for the moment. I opened my front door and noticed the answering machine blinking. I guessed it was Rashawna, wanting to firm up another sleepover.

"Don't worry about me tonight, Minnie," her voice chirped. "Joel and I have it all figured out. See you in the morning."

I'll just bet you do, I thought.

Seven

I set the tea brewing and headed to the bedroom to get comfy in pajamas and a loose robe. The kettle rose to a piercing wail as I returned to the kitchen and popped a cinnamon orange tea bag into my cup. I was glad to have the evening to myself so I could do a thorough rundown of the case before me. I grabbed a pen and tablet and kicked back into my recliner.

I used a numbered outline for the events of the past forty-eight hours:

1. Joel spots a suspicious character outside of the Dollar Store and wants to tell someone.

2. Suspicious character follows Joel and Rashawna to parking lot.

3. Trunk, rage, fish fry

4. While eating, we decide to go to police with suspicions.

5. No Detective Horowitz at station. Red shoelace tied to rearview mirror.

4. Dollar Store clerk Selena hauled into station as we're about to report shoelace

5. Joel declares Selena evil.

6. Rashawna sees mall stalker who may be Selena's husband and same person Joel saw — or not.

Looking at what I'd written, it didn't seem like much. Except for the red shoelace, this could all be a domestic dispute between evil Selena and her husband Joe.

Certainly the mall stalker wasn't alone among young men who liked to stroll the mall corridors, looking like they'd pick a fight in a New York minute. I resolved to talk with Selena at lunchtime the next day, and if I saw Joel, I'd send him to the fish fry to question Eddie, the cook. Even though Joel hadn't gotten off to the best start with Rashawna and me, he did exhibit a certain vibrancy, and I think he was beginning to genuinely care for Rashawna. Gosh, he'd wiped the shaving cream off her legs, after all.

I put the pen and pad down and finished my tea. That was enough for one day.

I had bundles of energy the next morning. It has always amazed me how the powers of the resting mind will tackle problems even when a beautiful man like Gregor makes another brief appearance in one's dreams. I woke up with a plan. I'd have Joel pick up lunch at Mack's Pier and toss a few questions at Eddie, the fry cook. I'd have Rashawna question some of the clerks in the mall shops near our space to find out if any of them had noticed the peculiar behavior of the guy in the mall the day before. I'd use my laptop to scour the Internet for any and all of the information available about the Red Shoelace Killer. I felt so good about my plan, I decided I deserved toaster waffles with butter and real maple syrup for breakfast.

I arrived at the mall at eight-thirty and had the surveys stacked and ready to go when Rashawna walked in twenty minutes later. She was alone.

"No Joel?" I asked.

"He's getting muffins and coffee for us," she said.

"As soon as he gets here, I'll lay out my plan for the day," I said.

"Sounds good. How many surveys do we still have to get?"

"We only need six, but I have to have them to the office by ten," I said. "Do you think Joel would be willing to help us?"

Rashawna sighed. She looked tired, and her curls lacked some of their bounce.

"Say, what did you and Joel end up doing last night?" I asked. Whew, thin ice here.

"Oh, Min," she said, tears welling in her eyes. "It was just awful."

Uh oh, this was bad. I put my arm around her shoulder. "What is it, Rashawna? Did he take advantage of you?" I said.

"What?" she said, growing more teary-eyed by the second.

"Hmmm, maybe young people don't say that anymore," I said. "Did he get fresh with you?"

Rashawna looked exasperated. "You mean did he put the moves on me?"

"Yes, I guess that's what I mean." Geez, Minnie, get the terms right.

"It's worse than that!" she wailed.

"Rashawna, for heaven's sake, tell me. If he hurt you …"

She collapsed into the survey taker's chair and laid her head on her crossed arms. Her chest heaved. "Oh, Minnie, Joel's a virgin!"

"What?" I gasped. "You mean you were the one who … he didn't try to …" I couldn't help myself, I burst into laughter. I had no idea how she found out this bit of information, but my imagination was tripping hilariously over a couple of scenarios. I did my best to squelch my mirth.

Rashawna continued to wail, and I was afraid we'd draw attention as the mall began to fill with shoppers. I found a tissue in my handbag, dabbed at my eyes and blew my nose. "Rashawna, dear, there are some things you just have to bear in this life. Joel has some quirky little problems, but I think he's basically a pretty good guy. Remember the shaving cream."

Her sobbing slowed.

"Maybe he's just taking it slow. It's been a little rocky with you two so far." I patted her arm.

"What if he's diseased?" More sobbing.

"I think your imagination is on overload. You don't hear of too many diseased virgins, now do you?"

That got a giggle from her. "No, I guess not."

"Did it ever occur to you that he could be waiting for just the right woman? It's been known to happen."

Rashawna raised her head and sniffed. "Well, maybe," she said, stiffening her shoulders and smoothing her hair. "Got another tissue?"

I handed her one, and she dabbed lightly at her eyes, pulling the tissue away to look at the dark smudges and assess the damage to her makeup.

"Give him some time. Four days isn't long enough to know much about anyone," I added.

"Okay, you're right, Minnie." She settled. "I saw in a new sitcom not too long ago that a couple actually waited two months before they, you know, did it."

"Well, there you go," I said with a mental eye roll.

"So, where is he with my muffin? Can he at least do that right?"

On cue, Joel the Virgin walked in with coffee and warm muffins, cranberry nut, it looked like. I had a brief vision of them sitting on top of my morning waffles.

Rashawna turned her head quickly away from him and wiped her eyes again. She struggled to appear normal.

"These muffins are huge," said Joel. He set the carry out tray on the table. "Hope you're hungry, Curly." He picked up a muffin and held it out to her.

Rashawna turned around and smiled. She reached for the muffin without responding to him, looking at me instead.

"Okay, you two," I said, "we've got a lot to do today. First, we absolutely have to get cracking on these surveys. Boss lady wants them on her desk by ten this morning or sooner. They were supposed to be in yesterday, but Deidre will cover for us until then."

"Can I help?" asked Joel.

"Just what I was about to ask," I said.

"I'm not due at the Dollar Store until after lunch so I can help Rashawna here," he said, grinning broadly at her.

Rashawna sipped her coffee and bit into her muffin. "After the surveys, then what?" she asked.

"Joel," I said, "I'll let you pick up lunch at the fish fry place where we ate last night."

"Uh, wait a minute," he said. "Why would I want to make myself a possible target for a killer again?" His eyes popped.

"Good question," said Rashawna.

"Well, we really don't know where he picked up our trail last night, do we?" I asked. "We had to go past the mall again on our way from the fish fry and back to the police station. He could have spotted us then. It's really a long shot anyway, and I don't think there's any real danger in broad daylight."

"I suppose you're right," said Joel.

"We'll order early to beat the lunch rush, and you can question the cook to see if he saw anything while we were there. His name is Eddie. Are you up for it?"

"Probably more than he was up for last night," mumbled Rashawna.

Joel ignored her. "So what are you going to put her up to?" he asked, jerking his thumb at Rashawna. He picked at the pleated paper on his muffin.

"While you're getting lunch, Rashawna can talk to some of the clerks near our hidey hole."

"Um, hidey hole?" Joel stopped mid-bite to look first at Rashawna and then at me.

"It's our pet name for this," Rashawna said, spreading her hands to indicate the small space we temporarily occupied.

"I like it." Muffin eating resumed.

"Anyway, one of them may have noticed the same guy prowling around yesterday. Did you two compare notes last night?"

Silence. Okay then.

"How about you, Minnie?" asked Rashawna blinking back fresh tears. "Did you talk to that detective?"

"I did, and Detective Horowitz seems friendly to the idea of us gathering information, so I'm going to do some Internet work and maybe check out one or two of the older editions of our local newspapers to see if I can glean any overlooked information," I said.

"Glean?" said Rashawna

"Glean?" said Joel as they eyeballed each other for the first time since Joel had come in with his muffins and coffee offering.

"A gleaner is someone who picks over a harvested field, looking for leftovers," I said.

"Oh," said Rashawna, "like Ruth in the Bible."

Joel and I stared at her.

"Aunt Lucretia knows her Bible back and forth," said Rashawna.

"You mean backwards and forwards," I said.

"Well, yeah. She likes all those Old Testimony stories the best."

"Testament," said Joe, "Old Testament."

"Hunh," said Rashawna, "I like that word testimony. Sounds more like you're really saying something with that word." She lifted her chin defiantly.

"Testament and testimony have the same root word," said Joel. "It's French and means to testify or make a will."

Now Rashawna and I stared at Joel. He knew about root words?

"Enough of this," I snapped. "We have about forty-five minutes to get these surveys done. Get out there and find me some takers." I shoved the survey forms at them and made shooing noises.

Rashawna set her muffin and coffee down, grabbed her headset, adjusted her face to charming and clip-clopped out of the hole as she spotted two women coming down the escalator.

Joel stayed back and drew close to me. "Min?" he whispered. "Can I ask you something?"

"Make it quick," I said as I turned my laptop on.

He leaned in closer. "Did you know Rashawna's a virgin?"

Eight

On and off for the next two hours, I searched the Internet for our killer. The *Albany Times Union* had an online edition with a Search Archives feature allowing searches as far back as 1986. I found the original headline and several of the follow-up articles in the months following the crime. I exhausted what they had. Next, I Googled red shoelace, famous murderers of the last twenty years and unique crime scene tokens. After all, the red shoelaces had to mean something. The things I found out were enough to give me pause. Everything I read brought me to the same conclusion: bloodthirsty killers aren't normal.

The scary part about it is they can look and act normal. A shiver ran up my spine at the thought of someone sneaking one of the red shoelaces into my car. It could have been a guy who looked like a schoolteacher, an insurance salesman or an auto mechanic. It may even have been a teenager, you know, one of those nerdy brainiacs who *keeps to himself. Nice guy, real quiet.* Would anyone have noticed him hanging around my car? Right in front of the police station, too. I shivered again.

I had to interrupt my search several times as Rashawna and Joel ushered in survey takers. That was okay, as it gave me a chance to come back to my own reality and put things into perspective. At nine thirty-five we had five surveys done. I sent Joel farther out from the escalator, giving him a clipboard of his own with the qualifying questionnaire.

"Try the food court," I said. "Lots of early shoppers stop for those huge frosted cinnamon buns around this time. Look for someone who's almost done with one, and see if they'll do it. Smile, be charming."

"Sure thing, Min," Joel said, sprinting off.

He was back in five minutes with a young woman who had short blonde hair, a stretchy black top, tight jeans and heavily made-up eyes. She was very pleasant as I administered the deodorant soap survey at top speed, and then I had fifteen minutes to get the lot of them over to the Chapel Marketing office. I noticed the blonde had stopped to speak with Rashawna after collecting her five dollars. I spoke to them briefly to let Rashawna know I'd be back in about half an hour. She smiled and waved me on.

When I got to my car I did a quick check of the back seat. After the previous night I wasn't taking any chances, even though it was a beautiful autumn morning, bright as polished crystal. I was relieved to have the surveys done on time, and I knew Deirdre would be happy to see me, as would Glenda, our boss lady. The office was in a complex only a few minutes from the mall. Deirdre greeted me with her perpetually cheery hello and relieved me of the surveys.

"Good job, Minnie," she said. "Glenda will be all puffed up and full of herself that these were done on time. This is a big account, and we don't want to lose it."

"I know Glenda is worried about so many online survey companies," I said, "but you just can't beat that one-on-one contact with the consumer."

"In spite of the partition," she chimed in.

"Right," I said wryly. "It's all in the voice, after all. So what's next for us?"

"We're looking at another study, this time for shampoo," said Deirdre, "but it won't start until Friday or maybe even Saturday."

"Oh, good. I'll be glad to have the next few days off, but I don't look forward to working this Saturday." I sighed. "Is there a chance I could pick up my paycheck tomorrow?"

"Sure, but it would be dated for Friday," she replied. "That okay?"

"It'll have to do," I said, turning to go.

Deirdre's phone rang. I heard an excited, familiar voice coming over loudly. Deirdre handed me the phone. It was Rashawna. Of course it was.

"Okay," I said. "I'll be back in ten minutes." I was chugging out the door before Deirdre had a chance to ask what was up.

I spotted them from a mall block away, Joel and Rashawna huddled, intense, and throwing furtive glances up and down the corridors. Joel saw me first and steered me into the hole when I got near enough for him to grab my elbow.

"What's up?" I asked.

"Minnie, the blonde? She told me the most amazing thing," said Rashawna, eyes blazing. I had the feeling that if I touched her, she'd burst.

"This could be huge, Min," said Joel.

"It so could," said Rashawna. "The guy, the one we saw yesterday? He's around here all the time. That girl told me a bunch of the other store owners and sales people call him the mall stalker."

It appeared as though Rashawna's and Joel's rift of the previous evening had been healed by the blonde. I was glad. At least I now knew one thing they had in common.

"Well, that saves you going from store to store," I said. "On the other hand, we might be able to learn more about him if we stick to our original plan. You've got this woman's take on it, but now that other store employees know we were asking about the stalker, they might remember additional details. The more corroboration we have, the better."

"Oh, man, another detective word," said Joel. "I'm starting to totally dig this stuff."

Rashawna giggled. "Sticking to our original plan is a good idea, Minnie. We have some time before lunch," she said. "We could still talk to some of the other store clerks." She swung toward Joel, curls bobbing. "Why don't we go together? I'd feel a lot safer if you were with me, too."

"I'm here for you, Curly," said Joel, puffing up a little. He ran a finger down her arm.

"That sounds good to me," I said. "Try not to be too obvious, though. The last thing we need is for this weirdo to get wind of our curiosity about him."

"I just thought of something," said Joel. "What if this isn't the only mall he stalks?"

"Yeah," said Rashawna, snapping her fingers. "What if tomorrow is his day for Stuyvesant Mall and then the next day is for that little strip mall with the cute earring boutique? What about that?" Rashawna screwed up her forehead as malls of all shapes and sizes came to mind.

"I suppose that could be happening," I said, "but let's concentrate on one mall at a time. It's something we might want to consider as the case builds against him, though."

"We're on it, Min," said Joel. He winked at Rashawna and took her elbow.

"Let's do it." Rashawna jerked her chin up and grinned.

I told them I'd clean up and get things ready for the weekend. I also wanted to continue looking at a few interesting links I'd found earlier while on line.

The red shoelace angle had my curiosity piqued. There had to be a reason, nutty or not, that the killer left this particular token. The link I'd found reviewed some famous cases and explored some puzzling tokens that other killers had used. One guy, who terrorized Chicago for several years, liked to leave certain cards from a poker deck at his murder scenes, like the ace of spades or queen of diamonds. There were rapists who left flowers on their victims, killers who hacked off fingers or toes, and any number of peculiar rituals that meant something only to the perpetrator. In their messed up little psychotic worlds, these tokens and rituals made the deaths by their hands profound and meaningful. It was morbidly fascinating.

Joel and Rashawna were back instantly, or so it seemed. My mind had been completely absorbed by my research, and I jumped when Joel spoke.

"Gosh, Min, sorry. We didn't mean to scare you."

"That's okay. I've been finding out some great stuff," I said. "How about you two?"

"Most of the people who knew what we were talking about were totally creeped out by the guy," said Rashawna.

"But that's the reason they didn't talk about him, too," said Joel, "like if they don't tell anybody they noticed him, then maybe he won't notice *them*."

"Except for the one guy in the Partyrama. He had all kinds of theories about stalkers and killers, even vampires," said Rashawna.

"It was almost like he hoped this mall had a real, live, sicko killer for him to admire," Joel added.

"He had that heavy Goth thing going on, too," said Rashawna, "so we kind of got out of there fast."

"Ugh, black fingernails," said Joel, making a sour face.

"Anyway, this guy got the nickname of mall stalker for a reason. I wonder if anyone reported him to mall security," I said.

"Well, that's the thing, too," said Joel. "He stalks the mall. So far he hasn't stalked a person, at least that we know of. Unless maybe it's me." He gulped.

"You're right," I said. "He can walk around the mall looking like Jack the Ripper, but if he doesn't do anything … hmm," I said. "Did anyone mention anything about his appearance that seemed unusual?"

"From what we heard, he has a real tough guy look, no smiling allowed, and his hair was dark and kind of all over his head," answered Joel, pushing his own hair over his forehead by way of demonstration. No Tonto bandana today.

"You know that could be about half the kids who are kickin' it around here," said Rashawna.

"Kickin' it?"

"Yeah, you know, Min, hanging out with their friends," said Joel.

"Yeah," said Rashawna, joining him in his light disdain for my appalling lack of knowledge in the current slang department.

"I'll remember that," I said. "Did any of them mention a strange-looking forehead? You mentioned that to me, Rashawna."

"That's right, I did tell you about that, but nobody we talked to said anything about it," she said. "If he kept his hair down like that, it could be accidental that I noticed it, and maybe nobody wanted to stare back, you know?"

"Did you see anything weird about the forehead with the guy who was staring at you, Joel?"

"No, but I wasn't staring back. Why give the guy a reason to give you an ax to the scull on your way out of work?"

"We didn't really get to comparing notes last night," said Rashawna, just above a whisper.

Joel squeezed her hand.

"Okay, then," I said. "That's about all we can do with this now, anyway."

"Time to go with the second part of our plan," said Joel. "Um, do either of you have any money for the fish fry?"

Joel came back with takeout from Mack's Pier and updated us on his talk with the fry cook, Eddie. I opened the slightly grease-stained white bag, and the heavy aroma of fried white haddock and vinegar soon spread like a mist through our little space.

"That cook guy says he didn't notice much of what went on outside his kitchen last night," said Joel, "but get this. The waitress we had the other night overheard us. When she gave me the takeout bag, she whispered that she'd noticed a blue truck across the street but didn't think much of it at the time. She said it had a missing hubcap."

"She must have thought something wasn't right if she even mentioned it to you."

"Yeah," said Joel, crunching away on his fish. "The blue truck reminded her of one that her old boyfriend drove for a while, not exactly new, like a 2002 Ford or something. She thinks the boyfriend sold it to Joel's cousin. She said it was across the street until just after we left."

"Did she remember seeing the driver?" I asked.

"Nope."

"I wonder if it would be worth it to go back and do a stakeout there," I said.

"Oh, this just gets cooler and cooler," said Joel, eyes gleaming. He picked up three vinegar fries and twirled them before popping them into his mouth.

"A stakeout?" said Rashawna. "Okay, now this is sounding like some made-for-TV movie. Are we supposed to be doing something like that?"

"From what you said, Min, that detective could use information," said Joel. "That's all we'd be doing, getting information, right?" He was so animated it made me smile.

They looked at me, and I knew they each had a point. Would we be putting ourselves in too much danger? "That's all we're doing," I said, responding to Joel. "Any real trouble starts, and we're on the phone to the police."

"Well, okay then," said Joel. "I'm in."

"Good deal," I said. "Now, if one of us was there for a few hours, say across the street, we might be able to discover a connection between the fish fry, the driver of the blue truck and whoever put that shoelace in my car."

"Wow, you make it sound like espionage or something," blurted Rashawna.

"I've learned a lot from reading great crime fiction," I said.

"I could stake the place out after work," Joel offered. He drew greasy fingers across his jeans. Like most men, he seemed to think clothes were made of napkins.

"I think I'll skip this one and just stake out that new reality show on TV," said Rashawna.

"All you'd have to do, Joel, is to notice if the truck turns up again," I said.

"And if it does?"

"Just take notes, who was driving, the license plate number, a description of the driver, things like that," I said. "Don't *do* anything. The blue truck may mean absolutely nothing. Notes only."

"No problem," he said. "Notes is my middle name. One thing though. What do I do the stakeout in?"

"You don't have a vehicle?" I asked.

"Used to," he said, "but I couldn't keep up the insurance payments."

"Hmm, can you borrow one?" We looked at Rashawna.

"Oh, no," she said. "I don't think I know a spit-hex strong enough to protect you *and* my car from some whacko killer."

"Spit-hex?"

"Don't even go there right now," I said, turning to Joel and raising my brows. "Rashawna, our suspect has no idea what your car looks like. If something strange and scary happens while Joel is there, all he has to do is leave."

"Yeah, and I could drop you at home now and bring you a nice surprise when I'm done checking the place out." Joel's eyes turned all liquid as he gazed at Rashawna.

Her face softened. "Really, what would that surprise be?"

"Well, Babe, if I told you it wouldn't be a surprise, would it?"

"He has a point, dear," I said.

"Well ..."

"I knew you'd see it our way," said Joel hastily, "and just think, we could really help solve this case."

"You think it's pretty safe, Minnie?" asked Rashawna.

"I wouldn't send him if I thought there was a real danger," I said. "He'll just be taking notes."

"Yeah, notes," repeated Joel.

They agreed to meet outside the Dollar Store after Joel got off work. We also decided to meet for breakfast the next morning to discuss his findings. In the meantime I had to spend my evening shopping for some of life's bare necessities, like food. I filled my larder once a month, and at that moment the cupboard was as bare as Old Mother Hubbard's.

Nine

I turned into the parking lot of my favorite grocery store, Hannaford, and checked my wallet. I'd have to use one of my credit cards, because my checking account was so low the numbers were huddling together for warmth. Getting paid once a month was no picnic at my age. My husband's small pension covered rent, utilities and a few other necessities, but I was on my own for food, clothing and earrings. Social Security couldn't come soon enough to suit me. I grabbed a grocery cart and headed for the produce aisle. I had a sudden craving for a big salad. I tossed a leafy bunch of romaine, a cucumber, some grape tomatoes, an avocado, mushrooms, and a bag of chunky croutons into my cart. Next, I hit the deli counter.

The scent of garlic, black peppercorns and pungent cheeses overtook my senses as I looked over the various meats. Moving along in front of the glass case, I noticed a vaguely familiar figure out of the corner of my eye: Selena. She was looking at the cheeses while the woman behind the counter sliced some turkey for her. I felt like everything was suddenly happening in slow motion, and I couldn't take my eyes off her. Her long brown hair just touched her shoulders. She had a nearly perfect nose, and her eyes were wide and clear, but there was almost no expression on her face or in her movements. I don't pretend to be able to judge strangers, but something told me Selena wasn't a happy or contented person at all. She turned her head in my direction, and I had a moment of panic. Would she recognize me as the person who'd bought all those Taffy Tales yesterday? The spices on a rack beside me were suddenly the focus of my undivided attention.

When Selena took the turkey from the deli woman, I glanced at her hands. They were almost like a man's, kind of fleshy with big knuckles. She said, "No, thanks," when the deli woman mentioned the Swiss cheese on sale, and then she came in my direction. I ducked my head into the fresh wheat loaves on a low shelf. There was the heavy scent of musk as Selena passed behind me.

I ordered my cold cuts and decided to follow Selena through the store as unobtrusively as I could. All I had to do, really, was follow the musk. Ugh, I hate musk. My slow motion state of mind sped up a bit as I rounded the cereal aisle and spotted her turning out of it. I quickened my step and caught my toe on one of those yellow Caution: Wet Floor signs, sending it clonking into the aisle. So much for being unobtrusive. A little boy laughed loudly at me from the high seat in his mother's cart. I righted the sign and reached the end of the aisle just in time to see Selena going for the frozen foods. Then I stopped myself. What was I hoping to accomplish anyway? I had no intention of confronting the woman, so what the heck was I doing? I slowed down and took a deep breath. I had shopping to do.

By the time I got to the checkout, my cart was full, about a hundred dollars worth of full; but I was all stocked up for quite a while, and I was glad the job was done. The bagger was pleasant as the plastic bags bulged over the cart, and he volunteered to help me out.

"I can manage," I said and thanked him. I'd left my car near the back of the supermarket parking lot, an old habit from the days when my husband insisted on it as a way of protecting it from runaway shopping carts. I popped the trunk and began to load in the groceries. My stomach was really rumbling now, and I couldn't wait to get home.

The last bag hit the trunk, and my ears perked up when I heard sharp words coming from a car about six spaces away from mine. I quickly shut my trunk and stood still to listen. I peered down the row of cars. Selena was screaming at someone.

"You know I can't go with you!" She spat the words out as she tried to open her car door.

I couldn't see the person she was arguing with. They were just out of the circle of light cast by the parking lot light pole. I held my breath and took a few steps toward them.

"You'll be next," growled the man confronting her.

Did I detect a hint of desperation in his voice? My heart was in my throat. Was this the killer? Should I intervene? Every instruction Dan Horowitz had given me flew right out of my head. I felt glued to the pavement of the supermarket parking lot. Gumshoe Minnie, yup, that's me.

"I won't, I won't be next!" screamed Selena and she punched the air a hair's breadth from the man's face.

"Get into your car." He exaggerated every word.

It surprised me that she did and that he didn't try to get in with her. Selena slammed the car door and turned the key. The car roared to life as she stepped on the gas and screeched backward. The man stood back quickly and watched her pull away, and then he walked in my direction. Uh oh. I stumbled backward, placed my hand on my car trunk, spun around and fumbled for the driver's side door. By the time he passed I was safely inside with the doors locked. Boy, some sleuth I was. I took several deep breaths to calm my thudding heart. Then I began to chastise myself. Why hadn't I at least taken a better look at him? The only thing that stuck in my mind was the yellow hooded sweatshirt he wore, hood up. I took several more breaths and was just beginning to calm down when there was a sharp rap on my passenger side window. I jumped about a foot, and my poor, recently calmed heart leaped into my throat.

"Excuse me." A female voice.

I looked through the window and saw a woman about my age holding up a grocery bag. I let the window down when I noticed she wore a store clerk's jacket.

"You left this on the counter," she said sweetly.

"Oh, oh ... thank you so much. I'm such a ditz sometimes," I said, trying not to gasp and blubber. I took the bag and watched her walk back into the store. She'd handed me my bag full of salad fixings.

By the time I got back to my apartment, unloaded my groceries, put them away and fixed myself a cup of tea, I was too tired to be scared. True enough, the case was becoming more complicated by the minute, but I just couldn't care about it for at least the next half hour. Unfortunately, my desire for a big salad had completely vanished. I crashed into my recliner, turned the television on low and wrapped my hands around my tea mug.

I don't know how long I slept, but black and white characters were prancing around in some old movie just before I woke up. My stomach was grumbling, too. I unwound slowly from my recliner and went into the kitchen. I had no energy to make the salad I was now craving again, so I warmed a bran muffin while the teapot was heating up for another cup of tea. The phone rang. I glanced quickly at the kitchen clock before I picked it up. It was 10:45.

"Min?" It was Joel. "Sorry to call so late, but I think I've got something here."

"Where are you?" I asked.

"I'm in the grocery store parking lot," he answered.

"Because?"

"Well, I was on my way back from the fish fry stakeout, but I remembered I had to stop to get Rashawna's surprise."

"I'm listening," I said. My teapot was about to scream so I reached back to turn off the stove.

"I was in the Hannaford lot and ..."

I was jolted wide awake. "The Hannaford? What time was that?" I asked quickly.

"About a half hour ago," said Joel.

"I was there earlier in the evening, and something happened then, too. Why don't you come over and tell me about it. I'm quite awake." I gave him directions to my apartment. About ten minutes later he was at my door. He rubbed his chilled hands together as he came inside.

"Are you a tea drinker?" I asked.

"Uh, not really. Got anything stronger, like hot chocolate?" He grinned.

"Sure," I said, thinking hot milk and some chocolate syrup would have to do. I split the muffin with him and got the hot chocolate made up. Then we sat on the couch and compared notes.

"I saw that blue truck again in the grocery parking lot," said Joel.

"The same one the waitress told you about, right?"

"Yeah, I'm pretty sure. I was kind of spooked to see it, but I knew he wasn't following me or anything."

"Especially since he was there ahead of you," I said.

"Uh, yeah. Anyway, it was a blue Ford and had a missing hubcap, so I'm almost positive it was the same guy."

"Could you see him clearly, anything stick out?"

"No, it was parked kind of in a dark spot in the lot. All I could see was his head."

"Did you get a license plate number?"

"No, it was too dark. I was sorta out there all alone, so I just decided to call you." Joel took a bite of the muffin. "I didn't see a thing at the fish fry place." He shrugged his shoulders. "I guess I'm not the best stakeout man."

"Maybe we can still call Detective Horowitz and tell him our suspicions."

"Yeah? What are you suspicious about? You said you saw something there, too."

"I saw Selena," I said.

Joel gagged on his hot chocolate. "Man, that woman is everywhere. What happened?"

"I saw her in the store and then out in the parking lot," I said. "My car was parked only a few cars down from hers. She was arguing with someone."

"No big surprise there. That chick argues with everybody."

"This was a man, and he was not very happy with her," I said.

"What'd he look like?"

"I had the same problem you did, too dark to tell. They were just on the edge of the circle of light there in the lot."

"What'd they say?"

"She was yelling at him that she couldn't go with him," I said.

"Really? I wonder what that was all about." He took another bite of the bran muffin and slurped down the last of the hot chocolate.

"Yeah, me too," I said. "Then he told her she'd be next."

Another choking sound from Joel. "Whoa, Min, this is serious. That might have been the killer right there. I woulda wet my pants." He wrapped his hands around the mug and crossed his legs.

"Well, I managed not to do that," I said, "but I did do something stupid."

"Oh, good, I'm not the only one then. What'd you do?"

"He told her to get in the car, which she did. Then she tore out of the parking lot." I stopped and took a long pull on my tea. "After that, he walked right toward me and I stumbled back to my car, got in and slammed the door."

"That wasn't stupid, that was smart," said Joel.

"Miss Marple would have figured out a way to confront him," I said.

"Oh, is she somebody you know from the police department?"

"No, Miss Marple is one of Agatha Christie's most famous characters," I said. Joel looked completely confused. "Never mind. The point is, I didn't even get a good look at his face. The only thing I managed to notice was his bright yellow, hooded sweatshirt."

"Did you see where he went?" Joel asked. "I wonder if it's the guy in the truck."

I looked at Joel. What were the chances there? What reason would the man who confronted Selena have for hanging around the Hannaford for two hours after I'd left?

The phone rang.

"Minnie?" It was Rashawna. "Sorry to call you so late, but I'm worried about Joel."

"He's here, Rashawna," I said, turning to him.

"He is? What's he doing there?"

"We're comparing notes about some things that went on tonight," I said.

"Huh, I'll bet I won't be getting any surprise tonight then."

"Oh, I wouldn't be too sure about that. We're almost done, and if it's not too late, I'll send him your way," I said.

"Okay, I guess I'll wait for him," she said, sighing heavily. "Oh and hey, do you have the television on?" she asked.

"I've got the old movie channel on," I said.

"Turn it to the eleven o'clock news, Minnie," she said. "They found some guy dead in the parking lot at the Hannaford store by you."

"What!" I waved my hand frantically toward the television, trying to get Joel's attention. "Joel, turn on the news." But Joel had his hand over his stomach. I said goodbye to Rashawna.

"Minnie, what kind of muffin was that?" Joel asked.

"Bran," I said.

"Where's your bathroom?" he gasped.

I pointed to the small hallway off the kitchen. "The door before the bedroom."

Joel dashed past me still holding his stomach. He threw the light switch on in the bathroom and slammed the door. I didn't even want to know what was going to happen in there. I went back to my recliner, plopped down and turned to the eleven o'clock news, moving the volume button way up.

The first thing I saw was the piece of a yellow, hooded sweatshirt poking out of a body bag.

Ten

There was no Gregor in my dream that night. I tossed and turned and worried. Joel had been too exhausted from his altercation with the bran muffin to leave the night before, and after repeated trips to the bathroom he'd finally conked out on the chair bed that had previously been occupied by Rashawna. We called her to let her know the situation, and Joel promised to pick her up early the next morning.

He stumbled out the door at about seven, and they were soon back for breakfast. I'd brewed a huge pot of coffee and cooked up a pan of scrambled eggs. I buttered toast and put out some strawberry jam while sausage patties sizzled in a second pan.

"I am so glad we don't have to work today," said Rashawna as she dug into the eggs.

"That 'we' doesn't include me," said Joel.

"Huh?" she said.

"You have to be at the store today, Joel?" I asked.

"In an hour," he said, pouring himself a second cup of coffee.

"You don't look so good," I said.

"All I need is some good food and a shower," he said. He slapped some jam onto a third piece of toast.

"Feel free," I said, gesturing in the general direction of the bathroom. I'd been up very early, and I'd already showered and dressed. Joel had slept soundly and just barely cracked an eyelid when the phone rang at quarter of seven.

Rashawna and I sipped and nibbled on the remnants of breakfast while Joel hit the shower. "So what do you think, Minnie?" she asked. "Is this case getting just a little too freakazoid, or what?"

I knew what she meant. My super sleuth fantasy life and my real one were walking shoulder to shoulder, and it scared the bejeebers out of me. Plus, I'd sort of dragged two excitable young people into the whole mess.

"Do you think someone's watching us?" Rashawna added quickly.

"It sure seems like it," I said. "My big question is why. Detective Horowitz says there's probably a connection we're just not aware of yet."

"It's just got to have something to do with that guy in the mall," said Rashawna. "When he looked at me it was on purpose. Like he was looking at me, Rashawna, you know, not like a guy who's just looking at a hot chick." She hugged herself.

"You know, if you're really scared I wouldn't blame you and Joel if you stepped back and got out."

"Get out of what?" said Joel, coming out of the bathroom. His hair was damp and curly on his forehead, and he'd had to put his day-old clothes back on, but he looked considerably brighter than he had a few minutes ago.

"Minnie says you and I should maybe step away from this case," said Rashawna.

"What!" cried Joel. "Sweet girl, this is the most exciting thing to happen to me in a long time." He leaned over the table and grinned at Rashawna. "We are on a case," he purred. "We are crack detectives, just like Nick and Nora Charles."

"Who?" Rashawna looked at him like one of his heads was on crooked.

"You know, from *The Thin Man*, the classic old movie. What an over-the-top team they were." His eyes glazed over as imagined himself to be the dashing William Powell.

"I'm impressed, Joel," I said. "I wouldn't have taken you for an old movie buff."

"I wouldn't know about any old movies," said Rashawna. "I only do classic MTV."

Joel groaned and dunked a leftover piece of toast into the dregs of his cold coffee. "Anyway, I don't think we should back out now. It's just getting exciting."

Joel and Rashawna had one of the most bizarre relationships I'd ever witnessed. Most of the time she was so prickly, I worried Joel would come away with stingers in his flesh with every encounter. Then, when he turned on the charm, she'd melt into little girl giggles and fawn all over him, like now.

"Did you think of me while you were in that cold car all alone last night?" she whispered. "I guess I shoulda been with you. A stakeout can be dangerous."

Oh, like she would know.

"It wouldn't have been too hard to warm to your form," Joel purred, "but that wouldn't have done the stakeout any good, would it?"

Deep mutual eye gazing.

"Okay, look, you two," I said, "we've had a couple of scares, but I think if we just keep it at information gathering, we'll be doing our part. We have the blue truck angle going for us—maybe—and a few other choice bits."

"I'm in for it," said Joel, pulling away reluctantly from Rashawna's adoring big browns. "I missed most of the news report last night. Was it our guy that got killed?"

"Uh, we have a guy?" asked Rashawna.

"You didn't tell her, Min?"

"No, I thought you might want to do that," I replied, reaching for the coffee pot.

"It was like something out of a cheap detective novel," Joel began. He covered her hands with his. "Minnie and I saw the same guy in the same parking lot with the same Selena last night. No, wait, that doesn't sound right."

"That chick again!" yelped Rashawna. "Is she everywhere, or what?"

"Anyway, we both saw him. I didn't see her, Selena, Minnie did," said Joel.

I was beginning to get confused, so I could just imagine what was going on in Rashawna's head. She flapped her hands back and forth.

"Wait, wait, wait," she said. "You were both in the same parking lot and one of you saw him, but not her. No, wait, is that what you said?"

I was close to crushing the coffee cup in my hand. "They hadn't identified the body as of the news report last night, so let's drop this part of the story for now. We'll explain it to you later," I said to Rashawna.

"Joel, maybe you could pick up a newspaper when you get off work today," I said. "We can check out the full report there and then go over what we have so far. Will Selena be at work today?"

"She comes in for the evening shift," he said. "I should be long gone by then."

"Come back here for supper," I said. "Rashawna, keep your ears open when you hit Macy's today," I said, knowing she never missed their Wednesday sale, whether she had any money or not. Credit cards ruled with Rashawna.

"Okay, Minnie," she said. "That sounds pretty safe."

They took off together with Joel's arm securely around her shoulder as he launched into an explanation of the parking lot incident. I silently wished him luck.

I always have the most energy in the morning, and I decided to use some of my time off to give the apartment a thorough cleaning. Cleaning was always my ally when I had to get my thoughts in line. Somehow, as I restored order to a room, my thoughts on a subject set themselves up in a logical sequence so I could get on top of the big picture. I began in the bathroom, since it had seen some heavy traffic in the last few days. I sprinkled cleanser in the sink and tried to figure out the confrontation between Selena and the guy in the parking lot last night. If he had been the killer, why would she have told him she couldn't go with him? A killer usually doesn't ask someone to accompany him to his secret killing ground, for heaven's sake. Usually he stuffs your face full of old chloroform-soaked rags, and bam, you're toast in the trunk. It also occurred to me that he'd almost sounded like he was warning her when he told her she'd be next. He was tense, and his voice was filled with, what, rage? Passion? Hard to tell, but he hadn't touched her. Maybe he'd sensed my presence or was aware of just how public a grocery store parking lot is.

The kitchen was next, and as I dumped coffee grounds and scraped egg bits from the frying pan, I considered the mall stalker. Lots of young women spent time in the malls, and that would be a rich field for victim selection. But had the killer picked someone at random from the mall? Probably not. The red shoelace tied around Jennifer Landis' ankle had to be more personal and targeted than that.

I loaded the dishwasher, wiped down the counters and decided what I'd fix for supper. Italian was usually a safe choice, and I could do up that salad I hadn't gotten to the previous night. I even had a loaf of crusty Italian bread in the freezer and an unopened jar of chopped garlic in the cupboard. If I had time I'd make some killer garlic bread.

I got out my biggest pot for the spaghetti, grabbed two jars of sauce from the cupboard, and put them on the counter. I had a few errands to run and wanted to have a head start on dinner, so I set the table, too.

On my way to the bedroom, I grabbed the pillows from the chair bed along with the blanket and sheets. I flung the blanket over my arm, tossed the sheets into a laundry basket, and hugged the pillows as I opened the door to the spare room to put them away. Something pulled me inside.

I had dubbed the eight-by-ten foot room my lifetime room. The closet was full of clothes that I couldn't yet bear to part with, like the suit I'd worn to my interview so many years ago when I applied for the assistant librarian position. It was a mossy green with a straight-cut jacket. The color perfectly suited my complexion. There was a pile of handbags on the shelf above the closet clothes rack, along with some books and a twenty-inch stack of old *Reader's Digests* that I knew had life-changing stories I'd just have to get to some day. Then the dress shoes, still in the original boxes, sat lined up in a row on the closet floor. Why in the world was I keeping all this stuff? Part of it was the smell. None of our senses has cash in the memory bank like a scent. Clothing and other personal items retain certain pungent odors, and they swirled around me. Standing in that room was like standing in my own history, and from time to time I needed to be reminded of what I had been, a woman with a wonderful husband, a house in the suburbs and a job I loved and had done well. A picture of my husband Marvin sat in a beautiful silver frame on the oak table next to the only chair in the room. Marvin had written his initials, MGM, in his own lovely hand near the bottom of the photo. In it he was on the verge of a laugh, and I'd snapped the picture myself just as we'd shared a silly joke. I briefly considered a sentimental journey, sitting there, wrapped in the blanket that was still on my arm, and going through the old photo albums lying on the floor. But no, I had errands and responsibilities in the here and now, so I shook off the notion, dropped the blanket on the chair seat, left the room and shut the door behind me.

As I walked into the living room, I glanced at the picture window. The sheers behind my drapes were closed most of the time for a sense of privacy but with some light still allowed in. My heart nearly stopped when I realized someone had his hands cupped around his face, pressing into the window in an attempt to see into my apartment. He must have seen my blurred figure because he moved back, waved, took a step sideways and rapped on the apartment door.

I unstuck my gumshoe feet from the floor and went with hammering heart to look through the peephole. Great. It was Briscoe Nichols, president of the renters' association. I cracked open the door.

"Hi, Minnie," he grinned. The man wore glasses about two sizes too big for his face, had a bad case of male pattern baldness and took his presidency way too seriously.

"Hello, Briscoe," I said. I noticed a clipboard in his hand. "Is it that time of year again?"

"Sure is," he said. "Hey, you look a little pale."

"You gave me a fright there," I said. "Maybe peeking through the window like that isn't the best approach."

"Heh heh, well, I knocked a couple of times, but no answer," he said, shrugging his shoulders. "Sorry about that." He looked at the clipboard, then me. "Minnie, we're trying to raise twenty percent more this year than last year for the rescue mission Christmas dinner, and we hope you can help out."

"It hasn't been the best year ..."

"I see here that your last donation was fifty dollars," he interrupted. "Costs for the Christmas dinner have gone way up this year. Is there a chance you could give a little more? I'm starting early before everyone spends all their holiday money. In any case, we won't be collecting the actual funds until the second week in December."

"Briscoe, I don't know. My income is pretty fixed," I said. "I'll have to think about it." I began inching the door closed.

"Mrs. Reynolds is in the same position," Briscoe said, "but she … Minnie what's the matter?"

He followed my gaze over his right shoulder. My mouth froze halfway open, and I stared at the truck parked across the street. Dang! I grabbed Briscoe by the shoulders and swung him around.

"You're coming with me," I said as I closed the apartment door behind me and stepped outside.

"I am?"

"Yes," I said. "It'll be safer with two of us."

"Wait, wait, safer? "His voice hit a soprano note.

"Just bear with me, Briscoe. I only want to get a few details." I put my hand out for the clipboard. "Do you mind?" I had my hand on it before he could answer. He reluctantly let go as I dragged him along toward the street. He scurried to keep up with me. I wanted to get the license plate number. I was almost certain this was the 1989 Ford that seemed to be playing a key role in the case.

Briscoe and I were puffing noisily when we got to the truck. "Do you know anything about trucks?" I asked him.

"Well, this one's old and blue," he gasped. His head moved back and forth as he looked up and down the street.

I sighed and walked to the front of the pickup. I wrote down the plate number and noted that it was indeed a Ford. I was about to do a walk around to see if there was a missing hubcap when I heard the sound of feet pounding down the sidewalk.

"Hey!" someone yelled. "What are you doing?"

Briscoe must have seen the guy coming because when I looked up, I realized he'd turned tail and was already halfway back across the street. Okay, now what?

"I said, what are you doing, lady?"

This guy was about twenty-five, average height, wearing a knit hat over his hair, a dark bit of which poked out along his neck. He was unshaven and wore a charcoal gray sweat suit. He didn't look happy.

I dropped my hands to my sides and slowly moved the clipboard behind my back. I feigned interest in the truck itself and even ran my hand over one fender. "Nice truck you have here. Interested in selling it? I'm looking at something similar for my son," I lied.

"Sorry, this truck is not for sale," he said, scowling as he opened the driver's side door and hopped into the seat. "You should have more respect for other people's belongings."

"I'm very sorry if I've offended you," I said, backing away.

As he roared off I began my humiliating walk back across the street to where Briscoe stood waiting for me, hands on hips.

"What in the world was that all about?" he said.

I removed the piece of paper from the clipboard with the plate number on it and handed it back to him. "If I told you, I'd have to kill you, and the only problem with that would be finding the best way," I said. I was feeling a little mean.

Briscoe took the clipboard from me and smoothed the paper. He was all huffy.

"Put me down for seventy-five dollars," I said. I smiled wanly and wondered where I'd come up with that amount in the two months left before the holidays. In any case, Briscoe brightened considerably when he heard the amount. His huff was gone.

"Oh, well, thank you, Minnie," he said. Then he leaned over and said with a conspiratorial whisper, "Whatever it was with that truck, I don't want to know."

He seemed very confident that he'd said the right thing.

"Thank you Briscoe," I said, winking. And you never will know, I thought.

Eleven

Back inside my living room I took a look at the license number. Now, if I were really a detective instead of a bumbling wannabe, I'd know exactly what to do with it. Something told me, though, that this truck wasn't the one. Heck, the raving loon to whom it belonged came at me before I could even find out what the model year was, and there must be hundreds of old blue trucks in the tri-city area. On the other hand, it had taken some pluck to go charging across the street like that. Yeah, pluck, that's what I had. So maybe I did have it in me to be something more than a former librarian and part-time survey taker, waiting to get Social Security. I sighed and put the piece of paper in the side pocket of my recliner. I had some errands to run and promised myself Taffy Tails and tea when I returned. It was about eleven o'clock, and if I left right away I could be home by one.

My first stop was at the office to pick up my paycheck. Then I needed to go to the library to renew the mystery I was reading, gas up my car and check out the cost of a cell phone at the local Radio Shack. I grabbed my handbag, locked the door to my apartment and headed for my car.

When I walked into Chapel Marketing, Deirdre greeted me with a cheery, "Mornin', Minnie! You just missed Rashawna."

"Really?" I said.

"Yep, she wanted her paycheck and asked about a job for her boyfriend Joe."

"Joel," I corrected. "Was he with her?"

"No, she was alone, and I told her I'd let her know if we needed anyone for the next couple of projects. Do you know him?"

"I do," I said, thinking there wasn't much to tell her about him. I knew three things: his name, where he currently worked and that he was attracted to Rashawna. "But not well," I added.

"Okay, Rashawna gave me her cell number in case we can use him," she said. "Here's your check."

"Thanks," I said, taking it from her. Deirdre promised to call me the next day with the details of the weekend project.

The library wasn't far from the Chapel Marketing office. I got my current Agatha renewed and picked up another while I was at it. I always like to have a book waiting while I'm finishing up on another. I left the library and gassed up my car at the cheapest station in town, then headed for the Radio Shack. I'd fought getting a cell phone for years, but since I'd lately found myself in the path of some bizarre characters, I thought I could at least begin to acquaint myself with the things for the sake of safety, if nothing else. A young male employee pounced on me the minute I stepped through the double glass doors. He was tall and dark complexioned, wore khaki pants with a crisp white shirt and a striped tie, and reeked of some god-awful cologne. I briefly wondered if I should mention the new deodorant soap we were surveying as an alternative.

"Good morning, Miss," he chirped.

"Uh, hi," I said, looking behind me for a much younger woman.

"You look like you need a cell phone," he said.

"I do?"

"Sure, that's the first thing you looked at when you came in." He swept his hand to the wall, where a confounding array of devices was displayed. He was right; my eye had gone immediately to them. I decided to take advantage of his enthusiasm.

"Okay, here's the deal," I said. "I think it's time I got one of these things, but I'm baffled about how they work, what they cost, size, color, everything."

"You have come to the right place," he said, beaming. "My name is Jimmy, and I'll be your cell phone advisor." He chuckled at his own daring wit. I also had the feeling that he was dying to try out his sales pitch on me, probably what he lived for.

About forty-five minutes later I walked out of the store with my very first cell phone and even more on my credit card; but thanks to Jimmy's excellent tutelage, I felt I had a fairly good grip on what cell phones were all about, and now I was a woman of the twenty-first century. Somehow it was exhilarating, and I couldn't wait to call someone, maybe my sister in Poughkeepsie. I was proud of myself for taking the plunge, and I patted the colorful bag the phone was in as I walked to my car.

I was home sooner than I thought I'd be, and it was a good thing, because Rashawna was standing in front of my apartment door, Macy's bags in hand, jiggling up and down like someone in dire need of a bathroom. She hailed me as I walked up.

"Minnie! Where have you been?" she yelped. "I have to go so bad!"

"I think you're a little early for supper," I said.

"Oh, I know, I'm sorry, but you're closer to the mall than I am, and I just thought I'd stop. Uh, could you open the door? Like now?"

As soon as the door was opened, Rashawna flew past me toward the bathroom, a trail of shopping bags in her wake. I followed her in and closed the apartment door. I put my library books on the seat of my recliner, hung my handbag on the doorknob, and put my Radio Shack bag on the kitchen table. Time for tea.

"Whew, now I can talk," said Rashawna, as she exited the bathroom. She smoothed her pants and touched her curls. "I don't know what to tell you about first, my to-die-for bargains or the mall stalker."

"Oh, that'll have to be stalker first, girl stuff second," I said. "Want some tea?"

"Thanks, you are so good, Minnie."

I put the teakettle on and left Rashawna pawing through her bags. I needed a trip to the bathroom myself. The kettle's piercing whistle began to rise as I came back into the kitchen. I turned the heat off and got out cups, teabags and a few Taffy Tails. I put everything on a huge autumn red plastic tray, my dollar-ninety-nine special from the Christmas Tree Shop, and took it into the living room.

"Oh, yum," said Rashawna. "I was just in the mood for a little something sweet." She dunked her orange spice teabag up and down in her cup, and when the strength was to her satisfaction, she wrung the teabag around her spoon and set it down. She took a Taffy Tail and began to unwrap it.

"So, you've got more news on the mall stalker?" I asked.

"Um, sort of," she said through sticky teeth. "Remember that woman who I was talking to yesterday when you got back from delivering the surveys?" "The blonde with heavily coated eyes, yes, I remember her," I said, as I tore the paper from my own Taffy Tail.

"Oh, man, can you believe those eyes? She's probably way, way over-sampling at the Macy's cosmetics counter. Anyway, she works at that new shoe store, All in Red, and she says the stalker guy came in and asked her about a really awful pair of shoes with," Rashawna paused for effect, "red shoelaces."

"Really?" I blurted. "What on earth did he want to know?"

"That was kind of the funny part," said Rashawna. "He didn't want to buy them himself, he just wanted to know if anyone else had been interested in them—the shoes, not the shoelaces, except we kind of know it was the laces." She looked thoughtful.

"Did he find out?"

"The black-eyed blonde told him she didn't know, and then she told me something else."

"I'm listening," I said.

"Well, it seems he's vanished." She swirled the Taffy Tail through the air for emphasis. "He's been in the mall every day for weeks and suddenly, the last two days, nothing."

"Well, that fits," I said.

"It does?"

"If the mall stalker is the same person Joel and I saw in the parking lot last night, then he's probably the one the police found dead a few hours later. He may have changed his tactics from mall stalking to confronting Selena directly. He followed her to the grocery store and waited for her in the parking lot."

"Awww, Minnie, I'll bet you're right. Joel said he stopped there to get my surprise and saw the guy sitting in the truck," said Rashawna. "He said it was hard to see his face. The truck wasn't under a light or anything."

"Has Joel got you all straightened out on that?" I asked

"Oh, yeah, he filled me in on the details. Like a crystal bell," she said.

"I think you mean clear as crystal," I said, "or maybe clear as a bell."

"Yeah, one of those." She took a long slurp of her tea. "So, is he the killer then?"

"No," I said.

"Wow, you sound darn sure."

"I've been going over in my mind what I saw when he and Selena were in the parking lot," I said, choosing my words with care. "The guy could have just shoved her into the car and taken off, but he didn't. It was almost like he was warning her."

"Good point. I mean, how many killers stand around in parking lots insisting their victims go with them? Let's get real here. So what was he warning her about?"

"That's what I haven't figured out yet. She just yelled, 'I won't be next'."

Rashawna snapped her fingers. "I know!"

"Okay," I said. "You seem darn sure of yourself, too. What are you thinking?"

"Maybe her husband hired the guy to scare her, you know, because the husband was the one getting the peanut butter knocked out of him, and maybe he just found a guy who looked scary or something. But then, who would have killed him? The guy, I mean, not the husband." Rashawna swallowed the last of her tea and frowned.

"Hmmm." I said. "There are a few holes in that theory. Why don't we let it sit for a while? When Joel comes with the paper, we might have more to go on."

"Good idea," she said, and then her face lit up. "Hey, it's time for girl stuff. Wanna see my bargains?"

"Sure," I said, "that sounds like fun. Oh, and I have something to show you, too." I got up and retrieved my Radio Shack bag. "Do you know anything about this text messaging that everyone seems to be doing?"

Rashawna let out a loud hoot. "Boy, do I ever."

Around four o'clock Joel knocked on the door, and Rashawna let him in, wearing her new skirt and top.

"Wow," he said, running his eyes over her body and letting out a low whistle.

"Glad you like it," said Rashawna, twirling for him. The hip-hugging electric blue miniskirt had a kind of tasseled fringe along the hem, and the bright white scoop neck, long-sleeved tee allowed for a lot of upper body exposure.

"It smells pretty good in here, too," said Joel. He slid his arm around Rashawna's waist and lifted his nose, sniffing. "Yum, Italian."

"Sauce's on," I said, turning my head from the stove. "Would you two like some cola or wine?" I was quite positive the wine would be turned down, so I opened the refrigerator, anticipating cold cola for both of them.

"Wine," they said together.

Rashawna giggled. "We've discovered we both like wine," she said. "Had some at Applebaums the other night."

"Chianti," they both said together — again.

I rolled my eyes and shut the fridge. Then I opened an overhead cupboard and pulled down three wine glasses. I had a small wrought iron wine rack sitting at the end of the kitchen counter, and I pulled one from my small collection of three bottles. "You'll have to settle for the Cabernet Merlot," I said. "I'm fresh out of Chianti."

I poured, handed them each a glass and returned to my sink to fill the pot for pasta. "Did you remember to pick up a newspaper, Joel?" I asked over my shoulder.

"Yeah, there was one in the back room at the store," he said, pulling the section he'd scavenged out of his back pocket. "I don't know if it's our guy, though."

"No picture?" I asked.

He spread the paper on the couch. The three of us hovered over page three. There was a picture, all right, but only of a body in a bag on a stretcher, along with a short police report. No release of the name of the deceased pending a positive ID and notification to the family.

"Well, shoot," said Rashawna, "that doesn't tell us a thing."

"Guess the news team got there too late to get many details," I said.

"Do you think we should call Detective Horowitz?" asked Joel.

"I don't know that it would do any good," I said.

"Yeah, what are we going to say," asked Rashawna, "that you were on a semi-illegal stakeout and then abandoned the scene so you could stop to get me a surprise? That the shadow in the truck didn't seem like a big deal?"

"Nothing was a big deal compared to getting that surprise," purred Joel. He put his other arm around her tiny waist and pulled her close, suddenly disinterested in detective work.

"I guess we've got a little more work to do," I said. The salad was chilled and ready to eat, so I went into the kitchen to get it. I pulled a bottle of Caesar and a bottle of Italian dressing out of the fridge and turned the heat on under the pasta pot. "Let's start on this great salad," I said, hoping food would divert their appetites from each other to my food.

Rashawna had curled into Joel's arms like a baby snuggling up to her mother. They swayed back and forth as the wine swirled in their glasses. I clapped my hands.

"Ahem!"

They jumped ever so slightly. "Oh, sure, Min," said Joel, reluctantly letting go of Rashawna. "I'm starved."

"Me, too," said Rashawna, fingering the fringe on her skirt and taking a big gulp of wine. "Smells super-delish."

During dinner I debated whether I should recall the incident of the blue truck I'd seen across the street earlier that morning. Since I'd pretty much decided it was just a random vehicle that happened to resemble another in a completely different neighborhood, I kept quiet. Besides, this dinner *was* super-delish as Rashawna had said, and I gave it my full attention for the next twenty minutes or so.

"Minnie, Joel and I want to thank you for this supper by cleaning up the kitchen," said Rashawna when we'd finished.

"We do?" Joel uttered an oath as I noticed his leg jerked slightly under the table. Rashawna grinned broadly at him. "We sure do, Min," he said. He leaned down and rubbed his shin. "I'll even get the teapot singing for tea when we're done."

"That sounds wonderful," I said. "I've got a beautiful lemon cake to go with it. Then maybe you can show me how to do text messaging."

"Who doesn't know how to do that?" asked Joel, stabbing a stray chunk of tomato from his otherwise clean plate.

"Minnie finally got herself a cell phone, Joel," said Rashawna. "It'll be fun teaching her how to use it. We can even program our numbers in for her." She got up and began stacking the dishes. Joel cleared the pasta bowl and dressing bottles and they were soon chattering happily while they moved around my kitchen. It crossed my mind that I'd probably have to hunt later for misplaced cups, bowls and dishes, but I was very pleased that they were getting along.

I retired to my recliner with the Radio Shack bag on my lap. I opened the box with my new phone in it and took out the instruction booklet. Oh, boy, I was in trouble now. Arrows and buttons and numbered instructions assailed my eyes. I had only a rudimentary understanding from my session with Jimmy, and I hoped my friendly kitchen help knew a few user-friendly tricks that would increase my acquaintance with the contraption. I set it on the end table and turned on the television news.

"… dead in the Hannaford parking lot late last night. More on that later as the story unfolds on the eleven o'clock news," said the anchor.

I bolted upright. "Oh, no!" I shouted. "Why are we always just missing important news?"

Joel and Rashawna turned from their kitchen duties and joined me beside my chair.

"Who did they find in the parking lot late last night?" I yelled at the screen.

Joel laid his hand on my shoulder, "I've tried that yelling at the TV thing. Never works."

"Seems like we missed most of the report," said Rashawna. "Now we'll have to wait until eleven."

Twelve

None of us had made it to the eleven o'clock news. The wine and the heavy meal had me nodding in my recliner at about nine-thirty, and by ten I was out cold. I awoke at midnight, and somewhere in my sleep-fogged brain I realized Joel and Rashawna were gone. I was covered with a blanket, and there was a note in my lap saying they'd see me in the morning. I dragged myself out of the chair, used the bathroom and crawled into bed.

I poked my nose out of the covers the next morning with visions of cell phones dancing in my head. Or was something ringing? I turned one crusty eye to the clock on my nightstand. It was seven-thirty and I *did* hear a phone ringing—incessantly. I rolled over, sat up and put my feet on the floor. I was amazed that I'd managed to put my nightgown on the night before, and I pulled it down as I wandered into the living room and picked up my new cell phone. I was pretty sure I was supposed to press Talk.

"Minnie? It's me," said Rashawna. "You up?"

"I am now," I mumbled. My eye wandered longingly to the teapot, turned upside down on the drain board where she'd left it the night before. "You're calling because …"

"Joel and I have come to a decision," she said. She was way too bubbly for me at this hour.

"And you can't wait to tell me," I replied. "Where are you?"

"At McDonald's," she said. "We're on our way over with breakfast, on us."

"Mffftt," I grumbled. "Okay, let me get dressed first."

"Sure, be there in five."

Great. I hit the bathroom and then went back to the bedroom and threw on comfortable old sweats. The teapot was near whistling when they knocked on the door.

"Come on in," I said as I unlocked the door to let them in. Our teacups from last night were still out, also on the drain board. I flipped them over as Joel and Rashawna hustled through the door. The pleasant breakfast smells of eggs and sausage on muffins wafted through the air when Joel opened the big white sack and began putting the food on the table. He whistled tunelessly.

Rashawna giggled and looked adoringly at Joel. Did I want to know what they'd decided last night? Maybe it was just a tad too early in the morning to hear their astounding revelation. I yawned.

"We're sorry for leaving you last night," she said, "but you were so sound asleep. Did you get the note we left?"

"I did," I said. I tucked my legs around the chair rungs and took a muffin sandwich. One day soon I'd vow to go off the junk food, but with all the trauma in my life lately, I felt justified. Besides that, it was yummy.

"So? Don't you want to hear?" said Rashawna.

I took a big gulp of tea to chase the bite of sausage muffin. "Ahhh," I said.

"We're waiting," she shrieked, "for each other! Oh, Minnie, it's so wonderful. No pressure on either one of us for intimacy." She patted Joel's arm.

I was momentarily stunned, not by the revelation but by Rashawna's use of the word intimacy instead of that other word. She was like some wind-up doll of wonder. The very idea that they were waiting for that intimacy after knowing each other for less than a week had me invisibly shaking my head. Oh, what the world had come to.

Joel ducked his head into his hot hashbrown patty and pretty much bit it in two. This was followed by a gasp and long, loud coughing. "Pepper," he whispered hoarsely.

"Oh, honey," said Rashawna, her brow knotted in concern. "Here, take a slug of this." She handed him a cup of tea.

"Thanks," he said, gripping the handle. He took several little sips and relaxed. "Man, whatta they put in those things? All I could taste was pepper."

Rashawna's cell phone rang. She talked for about two minutes and hung up. "That was Deirdre," she said. "They do need extra people for the weekend project, and I told her you could work," she said, looking at Joel. "We have to be in the office around ten today so we can find out project details and working hours. She said you should come too, Minnie."

"Okay," I said. "Let me hop in the shower and get dressed." I stood up and began to clear the table. "Did she say what the project is?"

"No, but it'll take about an hour of orientation," said Rashawna. "Boy, I hope it's not another Supercenter exit survey. Those are brutal."

"Might be a mystery shop," I said. "Those are kind of fun. We haven't done a blind theater check in a long time either. Maybe there's a holiday blockbuster with sheets, trailers and lots of merchandizing." Then I remembered.

"But Deidre also mentioned something about shampoo when I picked up my check yesterday."

Joel looked at us. "Hey, I'm feeling all left out of your business talk. I don't know any of these buzz words."

"It's okay, honey," said Rashawna. "You'll catch on. Let's go so Minnie can get ready." She swept the breakfast debris into my big swing top trashcan and gathered her jacket and handbag. A few seconds later they were gone.

I was glad to have the apartment to myself, and the shower felt wonderful. I let the steaming water pound the knots out of my back and shoulders. I wasn't looking forward to working over the weekend, but weekends meant time and a half. I'd need it if I was going to have enough money for my donation to Briscoe's rescue mission effort *and* Christmas shopping. I never spent a lot on the holidays but I did like to do well by my sister, nephew, one elderly aunt and a few friends at work. I toweled off, opened the bathroom door and stepped into the short hallway between the living room and my bedroom. Yikes, did I see a shadow pass the window? Briscoe, maybe? I quickly ducked into the bedroom. Could be anybody, I thought; I did have neighbors, for heaven's sake. I fluffed the towel over my hair. It was so short it was nearly dry when I finished. Then I went to my closet and grabbed my good black slacks and a dark green chenille sweater. I slid some lipstick across my mouth and opened my earring case. All of my earrings were stored in small, stand-up cases and arranged by color and kind. My jade drops were in the stone collection, and I took them out and held them next to the sweater. Perfect. The jades would do just fine. I slipped them into my ears and felt them swing lightly against my neck. I picked up my new cell phone and put it in my handbag, retrieving my car keys from the bottom of the bag at the same time.

Nobody was around when I left the apartment, and I hustled along to the car. The air had a little brrrr to it, and I wondered how soon it would be until we saw snowflakes. I liked winter but never wanted to see it come too soon. The traffic was light as I pulled out of the parking lot and headed for I-90. I glanced into the rear view mirror, and just for a second I thought I saw a blue pickup a few cars back. My heart rate sped up a little. I glanced again, and there it still was, the blue pickup, all right, racing up into the lane next to mine. Okay, the old heart rate sped up a lot. The truck pulled alongside me, and I got a brief look at an oddly familiar, but not very friendly, male face. Then he dropped back and moved into my lane and was right behind me. I looked at the road ahead and saw my favorite doughnut shop. I pulled into the parking lot and hoped the truck would continue down the highway. No such luck. The driver pulled in beside me, and the man turned his head slowly to look at me. He wore a black leather jacket and a black knit hat that was pulled down so low on his brow only his glittering marble eyes showed, and those marbles were burning holes in me. There were plenty of cars in the parking lot, so I hurried out of my car and went into the shop. The man got out of the truck and followed me inside. Now I was near panic. I went up to the counter where Doris, according to her name badge, asked me what I'd like.

"I'd like you to call the police," I stammered.

"Uh, excuse me?"

Doris wasn't picking up on my terror here. "The police! That man is following me!" I swung around to point to where I knew he would be standing, over my right shoulder, but he wasn't there.

"Where'd he go?" I looked the length of the counter but only saw customers slurping coffee and licking powdered sugar off their fingers. "I'm sorry, he was right here."

"You mean that guy?" said Doris. She nodded toward the front of the shop and I turned. "He did look kind of creepy."

The driver of the blue truck was pulling out of the parking lot. "I saw him follow you in and then duck real quick back out again," said Doris. "Maybe he heard the word police."

I let my breath out slowly. Had the whole world turned into Creepsville? The only thing that would return me to my normal calm self would be if I bought a bag of doughnuts. Jelly. Chocolate. Cream filled. I got four of each and hurried to my car. Rashawna and Joel would just have to help me eat them.

I set the doughnut bag on the car seat and buckled up. Doing something normal and routine like that helped calm me, too. I sat very still and practiced some controlled breathing. Suck in, blow out. The foggy brain panic cleared, and I began to wonder what the blue truck angle was. As I headed for the office I tried to untangle the threads of this mystery. How many people were involved besides the red shoelace killer, anyway? Were Selena, her husband and the mall stalker in any way connected? If the guy who was killed in the grocery parking lot was the mall stalker, then there was a connection, at least between Selena and the guy. As much as I loved a good whodunit, I often lost track of the characters. I put further thinking on hold as the aroma from the doughnut bag filled the car. I pulled into the Chapel Marketing parking lot and hurried into the office, where a smiling Deirdre greeted me.

"Uh oh, doughnuts," she said, eyeing the slightly greasy bag.

"A whole dozen, too," I said.

"Jelly?"

"Oh, yeah, and more." I thrust the bag at her.

"Okay, take them into the conference room, and I'll make more coffee." Deirdre took off for the utility kitchen at the back of the building, and I headed down the hallway. Rashawna and Joel were already seated at the big round conference table in the middle of the room when I walked in.

"Whoa, Minnie, you look upset," said Rashawna.

How could she tell? I thought I'd pulled it together pretty well on the drive over.

"A whole bag of doughnuts is the tipoff," she said.

I sighed and put them on the table. Deirdre popped her head into the room and announced fresh coffee would be ready in a few minutes. I sat down next to Joel and looked at the pile of paperwork in the middle of the table. Several other survey takers wandered in and took seats. About ten of us would be working on this project. Rashawna stared at me.

"So?" she said.

"It may be nothing," I said, "but I saw a blue truck again, and the driver followed me when I left my apartment."

"Oh, Minnie," gasped Rashawna.

"Must be the one we saw," said Joel.

"Yup, across the street and down a little from your place. We saw it just as we were leaving a little while ago," said Rashawna.

"We are so blue truck aware right now," said Joel.

"You and me both," I replied, beginning to shake a little. "Did you see the driver?"

"Nobody was in it. I almost didn't notice it, but a really sweet motorcycle was cruising by and went right past the truck." Joel gripped imaginary handlebars.

"Joel has an eye for beautiful, don't you honey?" purred Rashawna.

"Sure do," he said and stroked her arm.

"This guy pulled up behind me and followed me to the doughnut shop. Not a planned visit, by the way. I thought he might keep driving, but he pulled in right behind me."

"Boy, that would set my breakfast tossing," said Rashawna, her eyes full of worry.

"I wanted to be somewhere public in case he tried something."

"Did he?" asked Joel.

"No, when I got to the doughnut counter, he'd already turned around and headed out the door. I asked the counter girl to call the police; maybe that did it."

"Sounds like he just wanted to scare you, the creepy, icky, weirdo," said Rashawna

"Well, the creep scared me a dozen doughnuts worth."

Joel turned to me, ready to say more, but suddenly I didn't want to discuss the matter with others in the room. Some big eyes were on us, so I changed the subject.

"Where's Glenda?" I asked.

"Talking to the big cheese," said Rashawna. "They'll be in soon." She stopped and gaped at the two people who had just walked in.

One was our boss lady, Glenda. The woman with Glenda had the most astounding hair I'd ever seen. Apparently, it was made of glass. It was blindingly shiny and hung almost to her waist. It swung like a curtain around her petite frame and glistened as she walked. The contrast between the jet-black hair and her pale complexion had us all speechless.

"Good morning, everybody," said Glenda.

Nobody looked at her.

"I'd like to introduce Sybil Grant, who will be giving you the particulars for our project this weekend."

"Hi, everybody," said Sybil.

"Oof!" Joel let out the soft sound, and I tore my eyes away from Sybil to look at him. Rashawna had taken notice of his rapt attention to Sybil's ethereal good looks and let him know her displeasure.

"Sorry, babe," he whimpered.

"I'd like each of you to take a packet," said Sybil. Glenda retrieved them from the stack in the center of the table and began to hand them out. Just then Deidre walked in with a big tray holding a coffee pot, cups, sugar and a plastic jug of milk. Nobody looked at her, either. The doughnuts stayed in their greasy bag. Sybil looked around the table and then purposely tossed her head. "I think you've probably all noticed my hair," she began, favoring us with a dazzling grin.

Glass teeth, too. I tried hard to banish the sudden vision I had of Dazzle White toothpaste. Most of us smiled back. Rashawna hiccupped.

"I'm the chief sales rep in upstate New York for Brilliance Shampoo, and I've worked on this look for three years," she said, tossing her mane again. "The shampoo doesn't take that long to do this, but I had to let my hair grow." She ran her fingers through it to make sure we were paying attention. "We want to promote Brilliance Shampoo with a slogan that will have every woman in America wanting hair like mine. The manner in which we've decided to do it is with a short, ten-question survey in the malls."

"Why only ten?" asked Rashawna, piping up.

"We want it short so we can get the maximum number of opinions," said Sybil. "We also understand that consumers don't like to answer long surveys, and we need three thousand by Sunday night."

There was a collective gasp around the table.

Sybil laughed and held up her hand. "We only need six hundred from Roaring Gate," she said. "We have ten of these going on in malls all across upstate this weekend, and if we reach our goal," she paused, "you'll each get a nice bonus."

A pleasant murmur followed. I had to hand it to her; this woman was good. Bonus is a magic word for survey takers, especially with the holidays on the horizon. Suddenly we were all ears. A little extra effort, and I could have the money I promised Briscoe and maybe some left for me. Six hundred surveys? Bring it on.

"Take a look at your packet," said Sybil, holding one up. "There's a three-page printout in the left pocket. Page one outlines your display setups, page two has your two day schedule, and page three has a sample survey."

I was okay until I got to the schedule. "Do I read this right?" I asked. "We're working from eight in the morning until nine at night?"

"I thought that might seem like overkill to some of you, but we want to blitz the malls and come away with the required surveys in just two days. There's a lot riding on the results of this survey. Our mutual client has a huge investment here."

She mentioned the bonus again. What a big, shiny, smart lady this one was. It would be about twenty-six hours of work, but the reward was probably worth it.

"How much is the bonus?" asked Joel. Atta boy!

"Depends on how much you work," said Sybil. "If you do the whole twenty-six hours, you'll get a two-hundred-dollar bonus, fifteen hours, a hundred. Less than that, and it's straight time and a half because it's the weekend."

Low whistles and happy nodding now. A few dollar signs danced before my eyes. I could certainly psyche myself for a two-day marathon of survey taking.

"Our main goal is to come up with a slogan for the shampoo, and if you'll look at the survey, you'll see that the last question asks for a slogan. The slogan suggestions will be entered into a contest database, and a winner will be announced on television during the Super Bowl game in January.

"The Super Bowl!" Joel whistled. "This is getting better by the minute."

"Don't drag the process out, though," said Sybil. "We want spontaneity to be the key."

"Okay, we don't have a lot of time to waste," said Glenda, unnecessarily clapping her hands. "We'll give you thirty minutes to go over the rest of the packet, and then we'll do a few practice sessions, okay?"

Sybil excused herself and stepped out of the room. She was back in half a minute, rolling a tan-colored canvas bag.

The rest of the packet looked like the field manual for a major military offensive. Little moans of protest went up around the table as we all read, but that grumbling took a backseat to what happened next.

"Whoa, Mama," spouted Joel. His eyes and all the rest of ours were riveted on Glenda and Sybil, who had pulled several wigs from Sybil's canvas carryall.

"These," Sybil said, "are made of human hair." She glanced around the table at our open mouths. "Hard to believe isn't it?" She and Glenda held them up in their hands and moved them back and forth in a way that made the light shimmer off them. I wanted one.

"Huh," said Rashawna, arms akimbo, "my hair's as shiny as that."

This outburst, not unnoticed by Sybil, was rewarded with the lady's sharp attention. "Do you use Brilliance Shampoo, dear?" she asked.

Rashawna was aware of all eyes on her, and she twirled a straggling curl around her finger. "Well, no. Never heard of it."

"Your hair is quite lovely," said Sybil, "but with our shampoo it could be even better. You could be a real star out there when you're approaching people." She reached into her canvas bag and retrieved several shampoo samples. "Use this for the next few days," she said, handing them to Rashawna. "We'd like all of you to use samples, especially you girls." She placed a whole box of them in the middle of the table next to the doughnuts. Joel reached over for some samples and snagged a jelly from the bag at the same time.

"I'm very good with an audience, too," said Rashawna, preening a little. "I used to model."

"It shows," said Sybil. She returned her attention to the rest of us. "These wigs are for display only and will sit on head forms at your information tables."

One of the other survey takers piped up. "So this isn't a paid survey?" he said, pointing to a page from the packet.

"No," said Glenda. "Everyone who answers this survey will get a four-dollar coupon for one of several varieties of the new shampoo. In addition, they'll get a single shampoo sample to take with them and a chance to enter the slogan contest."

"That's a nice coupon," I said.

"It's only good on a three-bottle purchase," said Glenda.

"That's a lot of shampoo for a first buy," said Rashawna.

"Right," said Sybil. "That's why we're using wigs and all of you. We need to create a mammoth buzz that will get this product off the shelves in record numbers."

"Is this stuff hypoallergenic?" asked someone directly across from me.

"We have a hypoallergenic line," said Sybil. "It's unscented but otherwise the same."

"Okay," said Glenda. "If there are no other questions right now, let's do some practice sessions and then break for lunch. If you do have questions after that, come and see us." She smiled at Sybil and took some shampoo samples from the box on the table.

Our practice sessions consisted of asking each other the questions about Brilliance Shampoo while smiling and encouraging the takee to stroke the wig, which I have to say not only looked like glass but felt like it, too. We were also challenged to come up with slogans of our own so we could prod the survey takees, if necessary.

"Where should we go for lunch?" asked Joel. "All this wig stroking makes me hungry."

"Yeah, you hardly had anything for breakfast and only ate one of the doughnuts Minnie brought in," said Rashawna. "Let's go someplace with a good salad bar."

"Salad, ha," Joel fired back. "My stomach's grumbling for meat. A sausage muffin and one jelly doughnut doesn't cut it for this growing boy."

"Why don't we go back to my place?" I offered. "I have some salad left from last night, and I can reheat the pasta. It'll save us all some money."

"Saving money's good," said Joel, "I'm in."

When our half hour was up, we told Glenda we were pretty clear on the survey instructions and said we'd be at Roaring Gate at seven-thirty sharp the next morning. Sybil announced she'd meet us all there with the setup materials and wigs.

On the drive back to my place, I glanced nervously in the rear view a couple of times, but no blue truck was cruising along behind me. Joel and Rashawna were two cars back in her car. I pulled into my parking lot just as freezing rain began to fall. Not good. What we didn't need tomorrow was weather bad enough to keep people out of the mall, especially the women. On the other hand, sometimes bad weather increases mall traffic, because a bright store is better than a gloomy house.

Joel and Rashawna hustled up the walk towards me in a state of high agitation as I opened my apartment door

"Did you see him, Minnie?" asked Rashawna.

I didn't even want to know. There were just too many *hims* around lately. I hurried us all inside and shut the door. "Do I want to know if *he* was in a blue truck?"

They looked at each other then at me. "Yes!"

Thirteen

"Let's sit and get warm." I turned on the teapot, popped the leftover pasta into the microwave and got the salad out of the fridge.

"This blue truck boogeyman is starting to get to me," said Joel.

"He came right up on my bumper," said Rashawna. "You'd just turned into the parking lot, Minnie, so you probably didn't see him."

"I'm pretty sure whoever it is not only thinks we know something, but is out to give us a good scare," I said.

"Yeah, and it's working," said Rashawna.

"Do you think we should tell someone now?" asked Joel.

"Let me tell you what happened before I got to work this morning," I said, ignoring his question.

"Oh, yeah," said Rashawna, "you kind of clammed up about that when the conference room started to fill up."

"Hey, I just remembered," said Joel. "We left all those great doughnuts there."

Rashawna shot him a warning look. "Go ahead, Minnie, what happened?"

I cleared my throat and directed them to sit down. "Let me get lunch on the table first." I passed plates and food, and poured water over the teabags in the pot. While the tea steeped we picked up the conversation. "I already told you that I saw someone in a blue truck maybe following me on my way to work. Well, he did, to the doughnut shop, where I wasn't really going, but he kind of scared me into it."

"Oh, Minnie," said Rashawna, her face full of concern. "I wondered why you brought doughnuts to work when we'd already had that big muffin breakfast."

"I wanted to be where people were. So the guy parked next to me and stared at me from his truck like some demon from hell, then followed me into the shop."

"Geez, that was bold of him," said Joel.

"I went right to the counter and complained to the woman at the cash register, too, but by that time he'd turned around and left. He probably heard me mention the police."

"That right there tells you he's up to no good," said Rashawna, viciously crunching a crouton. "He's a creep and probably a coward, too."

"Did you recognize him?" asked Joel.

I got up to get the tea mugs. "Not sure. I think I was too flustered to think straight." I made a vow right there to start thinking more clearly.

"Woulda flustered me, all right," said Rashawna.

"Okay, we can't let these guys scare us," said Joel. "I think we should write down a report of some kind, like all the stuff we know so far. What do you say, Min?"

"That's a good idea. We've got perceptions and real clues that have surfaced over the last few days, and it's important that we don't let any of them slip through the cracks." I got up and went into the bedroom where I retrieved the pad of paper with the notes I'd written out before. When I got back to the table, I saw that Joel and Rashawna had made short work of the leftovers, so I gave the pad to Joel, and we did a little brainstorming. I began fiddling with what was left of the salad.

"Okay, how many suspects are we talking here?" asked Joel. He licked the tip of the pencil, flipped to a fresh page and wrote a large number one at the top.

"Let's put the blue truck right at the top of the list," I said. "There's a connection there, I just know it."

I watched Joel write "Christine" beside the number one. Clever. Stephen King would have loved it.

"And the mall stalker," said Rashawna. "I mean, he may be the dead guy they found in the parking lot last night—or not."

"Right," I said, "and don't forget Selena and possibly her husband."

"Put down total stranger, too," said Rashawna. "That blue truck could be a truck of another color."

"What?" said Joel.

"Like the horse? You know, the killer could be a whole other person that we don't know about."

"That's the dumbest ..."

"Just put it down, Joel," I said. "Nothing is dumb at this point."

"Okay, got 'em," said Joel "Let's do places and props next."

"Props?" said Rashawna. "What, is this a movie script or something?"

"Actually, it might help to think of it in terms of a script," I said. "Movie plots are often based on what real life criminals have done, so maybe it would help us to adopt that kind of thinking. It might help us see the plot of this mess, too."

"Right," said Joel, "like in that movie, *The Usual Suspects*, with Kevin Spacey. Man, talk about suspects. 'Course, the darn thing was awful hard to follow. Almost too much intrigue. Anyway, here's our basic situation. Two years ago a woman with long dark hair, she's young, is found strangled with a red shoelace tied around one ankle, dumped near a high school. Hmmm, why do you suppose it's a red shoelace?"

"Good question," I said. "In my criminology class, we learned that a token like that, maybe a playing card, flowers or our red shoelace, has great significance to the killer but usually makes no sense at all to anyone else."

"Must have something to do with shoes," said Rashawna, "like maybe when street kids go at it over a pair of high-end sneakers."

"Right," said Joel, "or maybe it's about feet. And who buys red shoelaces? I mean, come on, *red*?"

"Remember, though, they were on cardboard clown shoes, and you can buy them in the party supply section of the store," I said. "They're longer and thicker than normal shoelaces, too."

"Perfect for strangling," said Joel thoughtfully.

"Don't forget the blonde story and the new shoe store," said Rashawna.

Joel looked puzzled. "Uh, what did I miss?"

Rashawna filled him in on the conversation she'd had with the mascara-on-steroids blonde.

"So, we have red clown shoe shoelaces and weird leather red shoe shoelaces," said Joel. "Does our killer have a foot fetish, or is he a clown who breaks a lot of laces?"

"Maybe he sees himself as a clown because he has really huge feet, and the girls made fun of him in school," said Rashawna. "I mean, they found her by a high school."

Joel and I looked at her. "Way to go, Curly," said Joel. "That could be a good solid theory right there."

Rashawna grinned at his praise. "I used to get made fun of in gym," she said. "You should have seen me trying to play basketball. I know how awful it is to be made fun of, never mind the horrible gym shorts they made us wear. Plus, you catch that ball wrong, and there goes a fingernail."

The very idea of Rashawna playing basketball temporarily interrupted our brainstorming. Joel's face and mine suffered a kaleidoscope of contortions as we struggled to keep from collapsing into laughter. I resumed normal first.

"Okay, what we're dealing with now is motive," I said. "Maybe the killer got a lot of teasing, especially from a girl or group of girls."

"Ewww, girls in packs can be brutal," said Rashawna, shivering. Then she snapped her fingers. "I just thought of something else." She turned to Joel. "You told me that guy who sat and stared at you had huge feet."

"Yeah, he did."

"Clowns have big feet. You know, circus clowns. Probably fake feet, but really, really big, right?"

"Interesting observation, Rashawna," I said. "I think we're seeing a pattern of connect the dots here. A few things might be falling into place."

"I wonder how we can find out about the victim," said Joel. "Do you think Detective Horowitz would help us with that?"

"I think we've got enough reason to approach him again," I said. "The blue truck mystery and some of the other things that have happened would be of interest to him or whatever other detective is working on this old case."

"Okay, I've got some good stuff written down. What's our next step?" asked Joel.

"The very next thing we have to do is get through this weekend," I said. "We're not going to have a lot of sleuthing time until those surveys are done. We're not being paid to hunt a killer, and Lord knows we've got to pay our bills." I stood up and began to clear the table. "We'll inform Dan as soon as we can."

"Do you hear something?" asked Rashawna. She got up, adjusted her clothing and walked to the living room window. "Oh, man, look at this!"

Joel and I were beside her instantly. She'd pulled the sheers aside so we could see more clearly. Huge sheets of freezing rain and pea-sized hail were pounding the pavement outside of my apartment. Not good, not good at all.

As a kind of October surprise, the temperature dropped five more degrees over the next two hours, turning the freezing rain into huge, white flakes. By dinnertime there were six inches of beautiful, glistening snow on the ground. Joel and Rashawna had taken off right after lunch because Rashawna wanted to be indoors before it got really bad. I didn't ask where Joel would go. I decided to make the best of it, and after going over my Brilliance Shampoo packet one more time, I made myself a big bowl of popcorn and settled in to watch a classic old movie, the timing of which was downright eerie.

I arose from my chair two hours later, having been completely spooked by the elusive and terrifying character, Keyser Soze, in *The Usual Suspects*. It seemed someone similar had popped into my life, driving a blue pickup. Just before I pulled the picture window drapes shut, I did a snow check. At least two more inches. Great, just great.

Fourteen

The next morning the sound of a snowplow woke me just before my alarm was programmed to go off. It was 6:30 a.m., and I shambled into the kitchen to put some heat under the teakettle. I chanced a peek through the living room drapes and was greeted by a true winter wonderland. The sky was lightening up to a pearly gray, tinged with pink and blue, making me think the snow wouldn't keep us from our mall shampoo survey blitz after all.

The phone rang.

"Minnie?"

"Good morning, Rashawna," I said. "How are things by you?"

"Well, kind of snowed in, but the plows are out, and we think we'll make it to the mall on time. My plow guy will be here in a while. How about you?"

Rashawna spoke as though Joel was with her. Had they changed their decision, then? I didn't even ask. "Plows are out here, too," I said. "If management got the parking lot cleared out, I should be there on time."

"I hope people like to shop on snowy days," said Rashawna. "Kind of puts me in the mood for Christmas."

I groaned. "That's an angle I hadn't thought of."

"I'm always working the shopping angle," Rashawna giggled, assuring me she'd be at our survey station in time. "See ya."

I hated driving in the snow. I decided to give myself an extra fifteen minutes so I could get the stuff off my car and use caution on the road. I'm always on road alert after the first snowfall. Even when they've lived in the Northeast all their lives, there are still loonies who seem to forget how to drive in the winter weather. The teakettle blew, and I lifted it off the stove and poured the bubbling water over my teabag. I took my cup into the bedroom and dug through my winter wardrobe, buried at the back of my closet. I pulled out a pretty plum-colored sweater and tan slacks that would go very well with my favorite maple leaf earrings. Perfect for autumn.

Once dressed, I then had to find my winter coat, gloves, and a wool scarf from the small closet by my front door. I bundled up and immediately felt like I should be in one of those fat guy tire commercials. It was 7:10 when I said goodbye to my apartment and headed for the parking lot. I was relieved to see it had been plowed, although individual cars had been buried by the plow blade's snow spray. Mine was one of them. I fought through the drifts and managed to get the driver's side door open. I popped my trunk and rummaged around for my snow scraper. It was only the end of October, but I could tell this was the beginning of a long, hard winter. I just knew it. Or maybe, my optimist self said, the sun would come out in a few hours and melt early winter away. Yeah, I'd think that instead.

"Good winter morning, Minnie."

I turned from my snow removal efforts to see Briscoe waving at me from his front door, which faced the parking lot. He had a straw broom in his hand and was throwing it briskly over the snow that had piled up on his welcome mat. I waved back. "Hi, Briscoe."

"Going to work?" he asked.

"Yup, special survey at the mall today," I called. "Thank God it stopped snowing." In fact, the sun had broken through, and the sudden brightness reflecting off the snow was blindingly beautiful. Little diamond sparkles pinged off surfaces all around me.

"Have fun," Briscoe called back as he shut his front door. "Mother will be up soon."

I envied him going back to a warm kitchen, where all he had to worry about was if the morning paper would come and whether he'd have toast with jam or cereal for breakfast. Well, that, and what sort of mood his mother would be in. She and Briscoe had lived in this complex longer than anyone. I didn't know a lot about Briscoe and his mother, but if the tales carried in the complex were true, it was definitely a co-dependent situation.

I finished snow dusting and got into my car. It was now 7:20, and I hoped the ride to the mall would take only the usual ten minutes. As I backed out I practiced tapping the brakes, a good thing to know how to do in winter weather. That, and knowing to keep a light hand on the steering wheel, had kept me from plowing into many a snow bank.

As it turned out, the traffic at that hour was nil, and I arrived at Roaring Gate in record time, just as Sybil was setting up a display table. I joined her.

"I sure hope people don't stay away today," she said. Her glass hair was tied back with a huge scarf, yellow with white polka dots, quite chic.

"I was talking with my co-worker, and we think this snow may put people in the Christmas shopping mood," I said.

Sybil stopped and turned to me. "I like your attitude," she said. "What's your name?"

"Minnie Markwood," I said. "I've been working for Chapel Marketing for about six years now, and ... "

"That's fine, dear," she said, interrupting me. "Could you take the cloth out of my bag over there, the yellow one?"

Well, I guess a busy shampoo executive didn't need to be bothered with small talking to a lowly survey worker. I handed her the yellow cloth, and she expertly whipped it onto the table, making a swirl of soft yellow on top of the white cloth that had already been draped over the large, round table. In her polka dot scarf Sybil and her table looked very much in sync. The eye appeal was huge. I noticed a few of the other survey workers from yesterday were walking our way. Joel and Rashawna were due about now, too. I felt a presence behind me.

"Mornin', Min," Joel said. He had a cardboard tray with three cups of coffee in his hands. "Coffee?"

"Oh, thanks," I said, taking a cup. "Where's Rashawna?"

"Not sure, but I hope she gets here soon," he answered.

"You mean, you didn't stay with her last night?"

"Nope. We got Chinese and ate at her place last night, then she dropped me off at Sears and went back home. Said she was going to call a friend to plow her driveway this morning. I hope the guy showed up. It's almost starting time." He looked past me to another group of people coming our way. Rashawna wasn't with them. "I'm going to go call her," he said and sped off.

"All right, people," Sybil chimed to those of us who were standing around her. "This table is our main information table. I'll be setting up a few smaller ones at other places in the mall, too, and we can spread out and work among them." She swept her eyes over us and favored us with a dazzling smile. "I hope you went over your packets again last night and have the procedure down cold. You two," she said, motioning toward the two people nearest her, "follow me, and help me set up the next station. The rest of you can fan out and begin taking surveys as quickly as possible. Don't let anyone get by you. Make eye contact and smile."

This was standard survey worker fare, and I wondered if it fell on deaf ears.

"When you've got five surveys, return them to the station nearest where you're working," continued Sybil. "I believe in you!"

Don't clap your hands. Please don't clap your hands, I thought.

She clapped her hands, smack, smack! "Let's go!"

I groaned inwardly. Man, this woman didn't waste any time. I hoped some of her energy slopped over to the rest of us. The other survey workers began walking briskly in the direction of Sears, an anchor store at the far end of the mall. Sybil paused before following them.

"Winnie," she said, turning to me, "it seems we have a few stragglers." She checked her watch. "Will you take charge of this table, and when they get here, please tell them how we're set up? Then just put them to work. Thanks. You're a dear."

Sybil grabbed her canvas bag and sped off at an impossible pace behind the others, quickly catching up with them

"It's Minnie," I said to her retreating back. The hair bobbed up and down beneath the polka dot scarf as she marched forth. Gosh, what's in a name anyhow?

I looked at the table Sybil had just set up. Two of the wigs from the day before, one blonde and one a peculiar shade of red, sat on forms at opposite ends of the table. Between them, in the swirl of yellow cloth, sat an array of six varieties of Brilliance shampoo. Piles of brochures, extolling its virtues, sat in front of those. A big supply of the samples and coupons we were to give away sat in a separate box on the floor behind the table. There were two silver mesh boxes on the table, one each for the samples and coupons, and we were to replenish them as needed. A lightweight plastic sign stand sat beside the table with the product name and yet another shining head of hair on display. Some folding chairs were also there, and I decided to sit myself in one of them and finish my coffee. This wasn't as cozy as our hidey hole, but I understood the reasoning. We needed to be out where the shampoo consumers could see us. The mall was nearly empty, and I thought it would look good to have someone of maturity attending the table as people began to parade through the mall, even if my hair wasn't made of glass.

So where the heck was Joel? How long could it take to make a phone call? Almost as soon as I thought it, I heard fast feet coming my way.

"Min," Joel gasped as he gained the table. "She's not answering her phone. I called her just before I left to come here, and the plow guy was coming down her road. That was forty-five minutes ago!"

"Well, okay," I said calmly. "It takes some time to plow out where she is. Her driveway is kind of long. Let's give her another half hour."

"You think she's okay?"

"Probably, and knowing Rashawna, she'll be going extra slow in this snow." I was using my librarian voice again along with a reassuring smile. "Right now, we've got to get cracking on these surveys. Do you have your packet?"

"It's under the table. I was here earlier, even before you, and helped Sybil set up." He took a bag from under the table and retrieved his survey forms. Some clipboards were under the table, too, and he shoved some forms into one and went to stand at the bottom of the escalator. He had a long view of the mall corridors there and could keep an eagle eye out for Rashawna that way.

I turned away from him when I heard someone utter a soft "Wow." A young girl and her mother had come up to the display table and were stroking the blonde wig. Okay, my coffee break was over, and I broke into my spiel.

"Believe it or not, that's real hair," I said, smiling and inclining my head.

"I told you, Mom," said the girl. "Did the shampoo make it like this?"

"It sure did," I said. "Brilliance shampoo is so new it's barely in the stores yet. It's also a unique product, not only for the shine you'll enjoy, but it cleans out more kinds of dirt than any of the other leading shampoos." Boy, I was good. "If you have the time, we'd appreciate it if you'd fill out a short survey and give us your idea of a great slogan for this new product. The winner of the slogan contest will be announced at the Super Bowl in January. Prizes include a trip to New York City, a spa visit and three thousand dollars."

"Awesome!" The girl held her hand out for a survey. "I've got a great one."

"Wonderful," I said. "We also have some small thank you gifts for you." Mother and child were putty in my hands. I reached into the silver mesh basket and took out some samples. Note to self: Grab a few to take home later.

They each answered a survey, and thirty minutes later I had theirs and eight more to my credit. The mall was slowly filling with shoppers, and the wigs were a huge draw. I appreciated the genius who thought of them. About an hour later I finally had a brief respite and looked through some of the slogans.

Brilliance! Got it?

Brilliance, first your hair, then your brain! Oh, brother.

I use Brilliance, do you? This one included a suggestion that a Persian cat be featured.

I sighed and put the surveys safely away, then looked over at the escalator to check on Joel. I was surprised to see no one there. I hoped he had wandered in search of more survey takers, but my gut told me he was on a Rashawna hunt. She still hadn't put in an appearance, and now I, too, was concerned. Could her crusty little car have finally conked out? But she would have called if that had happened. Suddenly I heard the strains of *Moonlight Sonata* coming from my handbag, where I'd set it near the back end of the information table. I fished around in it until I found my cell and flipped it open.

"Hello?"

"I can't find her, Min." Joel's voice was just a notch below total panic.

"Where are you?" I asked. Sybil would be at this end of the mall soon, and I didn't want her to find us falling down on the job.

"I'm staring at a gray wig at the other end of the mall," he said. "Sybil just left here and is headed back your way. I have twelve surveys, and she told me to take a short break."

"Joel," I said, a warning in my voice, "I hope you're not going to do what I think you're going to do."

"I'll be back in half an hour. The city bus will drop me two blocks from her place," he said and hung up before I could say anything else. Great. If these two screwed up my bonus, arghh! And here I'd been worried about a little snow.

I looked at my watch. It was 11:45. We had a lunch break coming up, and I still hadn't seen Joel. I was sick with worry. The Chapel Marketing team had collected only a hundred surveys, and our shining Sybil was getting nervous. We'd have to really hustle in the afternoon to get to our goal of three hundred today. Sybil had wanted even more, because Saturday typically has many more shoppers than Sunday. She paced in front of me.

"Is Joel still at the other end of the mall?" she asked. "Maybe he's got more for us. He's such a charmer, an excellent survey taker," she said. Was she simpering?

"Uh," I stammered. I had no idea what to say, but since I didn't really know if he'd somehow turned up in the other end of the mall, I decided to risk affirming that he was there. "That's probably where he is," I said. Then I heard my ring tone again. Dang!

"What's that?" asked Sybil.

"Heh, my cell," I answered, grabbing my handbag and pulling out the phone. I looked at the display. It was Joel. He'd programmed his and Rashawna's numbers into my phone the night I got it. "Probably my mom," I said.

Sybil frowned. "Your Mom's still alive?" Like I was the oldest person on earth! I favored her with a withering look. "Or not," I said. "I'll call her, or whoever, back."

Now I was frantic to get away from the table and looked around for a suitable place to grab a sandwich. "I'll be back," I said to Sybil. "We have a half hour?"

"Yes, you do," she said. "I brought a salad; I'll have it here. Enjoy." She dismissed me with her hand as she leaned behind the round table to grab her bag.

I hoped to catch Joel before he did anything really stupid.

"Winnie," said Sybil, calling me back, "why don't you take some of these with you in case you encounter any opportunities at lunch." She held out my clipboard, and I tried to smile as I took it. I didn't even bother to correct her about my name.

I hurried along to the food court. There was no line at Bobby's Southern Chicken, so I ordered the Spicy BBQ Bun with onion rings and a sparkling water. Then I took it to the furthest table I could find. I pressed Joel's number, and he answered on the first ring.

"Yeah," he said, sounding out of breath.

"Joel, where are you?" I asked.

"Right here," he said and sat down in front of me.

I jumped a little. "You look like you're being chased by the devil himself," I said.

"I got to her place, Min. The driveway wasn't plowed, but there were tire marks in the snow, and her car was still there. And the front door was open—you know, not locked—when I went in to look for her."

My stomach lurched. "Could you tell anything from the size of the tire marks?" I asked, fearing the worst.

"Classic pickup truck, Min," he said. "Do you think …?"

He didn't have time to finish the thought before his cell phone rang. He answered in one breath. I could hear her shrieking on the other end. Rashawna sounded terrified. Joel's face drained to a ghastly gray and I heard another, deeper, voice shouting. Then Joel hung up.

I reached for his hand across the table. "Joel?" He came back from whatever horrible place his mind had taken him. "What did she say?"

"She was freaking Min, like screaming, but she said something real fast, too," he said. "BTO 843. Then somebody yelled and slammed the phone out of her hand."

"We've got to get out of here," I said. "Come on." I dumped my Spicy BBQ Bun in a nearby trashcan and hurried back through the food court with Joel on my heels. I spotted two of the younger survey workers and waved them down. "Hi, I'm Minnie and this is Joel. We were all in training together yesterday." I smiled through my heaving ribs and waited for a sign of recognition from one of them.

"Yeah, we saw you," said the blonde. "My name is Tara, and this here is Brenda." Brenda was also blonde, but dirtier, and a gum chewer. She was really working her jaw but managed to throw a flirtatious smile at Joel anyway.

"We have an emergency to attend to," I told them. "I'll give you half my bonus if you two cover for us while we're gone."

"How'er we gonna do that?" asked Tara.

"When you see Sybil, tell her we're working another part of the mall," I said, "but only if she asks."

"Yeah? What if we don't get the quota and don't get the bonus?" asked Brenda.

"That's a lotta extra work for maybe nothing," Tara chimed in.

I'd noticed earlier that these two had had plenty of time for chats and coffee between surveys, and I decided to play on that. "Look," I said, "you've got plenty of energy and time to hustle these surveys. Less time for lattes and more time for shampoo surveys is how you have to think. What you're looking at here is your own bonus and half of mine. Where else can you make that kind of money in one weekend? Think of the shoes or CDs you could buy."

"Ladies," said Joel, coming to my aid, "you can have half of my bonus, too. You'll each have to work double quick, but," and here he paused to slide between them, wrapping an arm around each of their shoulders, "consider it an invigorating challenge. These shoppers are in great need of this shampoo and don't even know it." He squeezed the shoulders and broke out a killer smile. "They need to be informed about our product so they can be as beautiful as you are. I mean, look at your glory here." The clincher was Joel touching each of their heads lightly as though it were an almost unbearable pleasure.

That did it. Giggling like schoolgirls, the two of them promised to get the job done and to give Sybil the glib tongue, if necessary.

Joel and I took off for the mall exit.

Fifteen

We headed into the parking lot at a good clip and found my car. My chest was heaving only a little as I yanked the driver's side door open. All this fear and dashing around was doing a number on me. I could almost feel the calories burning.

"Do we have a plan?" asked Joel as he slammed into the passenger seat.

"We're going to her house first," I replied, snapping my seatbelt on.

"Why aren't we calling the police?"

That was an excellent question. We could put Dan on the alert, but I kind of wanted to get the lay of the land myself. Also, I wondered if there was enough to tell him. My mind was a jumble of wondering and worry, but all we had was a person who had been missing for just about an hour and a phone call that lasted maybe forty seconds. Plus, we had no clue of where Rashawna had called from. "We will," I said, "as soon as we have something."

Joel stared at me as he buckled himself into the passenger seat. "Uh, you don't think we have something?"

I began to shake a little. Here we go again, flying by the seat of our pants with panic and fear our only allies. "Any idea about the BTO 843?" I asked, trying to focus my thoughts. "Are you sure that's what she said?"

"Yeah, I'm sure," said Joel. "I wrote it right here." He held up his palm with the letters and numbers written in survey pen. "It might be an apartment number, or wait!" Joel snapped his fingers. "Maybe it's a license plate number. It's gotta be that. Now that I think about it, it did kind of sound like she was in a vehicle. "

"Okay, how's this?" I said. "We'll do a complete and careful search of her house. Maybe she wrote the number down or left us some other clues. If she saw the guy coming up the driveway, she might have had sense enough to leave us something useful." I backed out of the parking space and drove toward the nearest mall exit.

Joel groaned, and I knew what he was thinking. Rashawna had probably been fluffing her curls or smoothing her pants right up to the minute the guy grabbed her. If the number she had given Joel was a plate number, though, it would be easy enough to trace. That would be a solid lead to take to Dan. I cruised along the highway as fast as I dared, growing more cautious as we got into the less populated area where Rashawna lived. Then we approached the end of her driveway.

"Man, look at that," Joel said. "The guy must have hauled ass out of here."

The snow had been gouged down to the gravel that covered the driveway. Dirty snow chunks and gravel were mixed in with deep tire tracks. I decided not to park in the driveway in case the tire prints were of some importance. "I'll park back here, and we'll walk alongside the driveway," I said.

Joel had the passenger side door open before I even stopped the car. He slipped and slid up the side of the driveway, being careful not to mark up any evidence without further instruction from me. I got out of the car and followed him.

"Look at this, Min," he said, pointing to a spot that had seen some recent action. It looked as though someone had put up quite a struggle while being dragged through the snow. Joel bent over and picked something up. "It's a teabag," he said turning it over in his hand. "Huh."

It didn't seem like much, but I'd watched enough crime scene television to know that even the most obscure item could be crime scene evidence. "Don't over-handle it, Joel," I said. "Let me put it in my handbag. It might have fingerprints on it or something." He handed the teabag to me, and I found a tissue in my purse to wrap it. Then we walked toward the house. I followed him and kept an eye out for more—what? I didn't even know.

We pushed Rashawna's front door open and stepped cautiously inside. Her handbag was on a chair near the door, and the room smelled of her shampoo, maybe the coconut scented sample she'd taken yesterday. My eyes stung a little when I thought of her in the hands of some lunatic who would not be charmed by her little idiosyncrasies. I forced myself to focus on our task. Beyond the front room there wasn't much to see. I looked for a pad and pencil or pen on the telephone table by the stairs, but there was nothing written anywhere.

Joel came out of the kitchen holding a mug. "This must be what she had her tea in this morning," he said, sniffing it. "There's still some left in the bottom of the cup. It's her favorite orange spice." He gripped it tightly, and his jaw went to granite.

"I don't see anything here, Joel," I said. "I think we need some expert advice. Dan would at least be able to help us with filing a missing persons report, and Rashawna did say something about a blue truck. Is there a way to trace cell phone calls?" I'd made up my mind we were out of our depth and opened my handbag to get my cell as we turned to leave.

We stepped out into the cold just in time to hear the screaming. Through the line of trees beside Rashawna's driveway, we could see someone running toward us.

Joel squinted through the glare from the snow, let out a yell, and ran as fast as he could to her. "Rashawna!"

She turned into the driveway, staggered through the snow and collapsed into his arms. He reared back a bit from the jolt but steadied himself and held on.

"Just get her inside," I said to Joel. "She may be in shock." I pushed the front door wide.

Joel half carried, half dragged, Rashawna through the front door and into the living room, where he deposited her on the couch and bundled her in the old afghan lying across the arm. "Oh, babe, you had us so scared. You want some water or something?" His face was a perfect picture of fear and concern.

"No," she said. Her breathing was jagged, and her chest heaved erratically. When she'd calmed down a bit she spoke. "Just sit by me." She pulled the afghan around her and looked at me. "Minnie?"

"What can I do?" I asked. "Are you okay? What on earth happened?"

"Sit on the other side here, Minnie," she said, patting the couch cushion. "I need to be with safe people just for a minute." Then she began to sob quietly. Seeing her like this had a profound effect on Joel. Something in his demeanor changed, and it occurred to me that I wouldn't want to be her abductor and have Joel catch up with me.

I took a few minutes to look Rashawna over. Her eyes were a mascara-streaked mess, and her hair was wild, but I couldn't see if she was injured in any way. She may have had bruise marks on her arms if she'd been grabbed, but I decided to wait until she told her whole story to find out. I did notice and wonder about some faint red streaks, I hoped not blood, on one side of her sweater. I couldn't see her hands; they were tucked under the afghan.

Joel fussed like an old woman and patted her arm incessantly. We sat with her quietly for about ten minutes, and then I couldn't stand it any longer. "Rashawna, you have to tell us what happened. We need to call the police and give a report."

"I don't think we better do that, Min," she said. "This guy is big trouble, bad business, your worst nightmare."

"Uh, okay, sweetie, I think we get it. Just tell us what happened." Joel put his arm around her and encouraged her with his eyes.

"I was standing by the window, waiting for my plow guy, and I saw this blue truck pull up," she began. "I had a cup of tea in my hand, and I just about wet my pants. It was a blue truck again, and I went a little crazy, I guess. I'm starting to see blue trucks in my sleep." She inhaled deeply, fighting for control.

I could only imagine her fright. Her house was quite isolated, and she was like a sitting duck out here, with nowhere to flee but into the woods.

"I tried to think who to call, but I got all jerky and couldn't find my cell. So I ran to the kitchen and grabbed a knife out of the drawer. But then nothing happened. I didn't hear the truck, and nobody came to the door. All that quiet was scarier than seeing the truck."

"We found a teabag in the driveway," said Joel, interrupting her.

"You found my clue?"

"That was a clue?" I asked. I was very glad we'd kept the thing.

"Yeah," she said. "I took the knife and crawled up to the window. I saw the plate number on the truck. It was BTO 843. Then I thought that was like orange teabag, only backwards. And the 843? It's part of my cell number."

Joel and I looked at each other. Only Rashawna, our eyes seemed to say.

"So, I went back to the kitchen to get my teabag, you know, to leave for a clue for you guys, but when I turned around, the guy was right there in the kitchen." At this, she began to shake and sob again. "I didn't even hear him, the sneaky creep-o. I feel so stupid!"

Joel pried her off his shoulder. "Honey, did you get a good look at him?"

"Yeah," she sobbed, "and I didn't like it! What I can't figure out is how he found my house."

"I wonder if …" I said and then had a blinding flash. There *had* been a car just outside her driveway a few nights ago. That the killer may have followed us to her house the night we went to the police station was looking like a distinct possibility.

"What, Min?" asked Joel.

"Nothing, really, just an odd thought." I looked at Rashawna. "So this man was a complete stranger? You never saw him before?"

Rashawna blinked and sat up with a jolt. "Maybe he's that mall stalker," she gasped.

"Could you identify him?" I asked.

"Yeah, I'm pretty sure I could," she said and scowled, thinking, "but he's not the same guy I saw in the mall the other day. I would have recognized him from there. So there's another scary pickle in this barrel, it looks like."

Joel snickered. "I love the way you think."

I got up. "Okay, that does it, we're going to the police."

"No," Rashawna shrieked, "you can't! He's still back there in his truck. I think I killed him!"

Sixteen

"Rashawna, what did you do with the knife?" I asked. She looked at me, bewildered."The one you got from the kitchen when the truck first pulled into the driveway."

"I think it's still stuck in him," she said.

"Okay, back up, and tell us what happened before you stuck the knife in him," I urged.

"Okay, I'm calm now," she said, breathing deeply and smiling halfway. "This is what I remember. I had my cell in my jacket and punched six when he wasn't looking." She looked at Joel, wide-eyed. "I was so glad you answered! I only got a few hollers in but when he saw me and reached to slam the phone out of my hand, we hit a big icy patch on the road, and the truck swerved bad. He was all distracted, so I took the knife out of my sleeve and stabbed him in the neck." She pulled her hands from beneath the afghan and stared at them. "Is that blood?"

Joel and I recoiled together. Joel shook his head and spoke first. "Okay, kiddo, I want you to focus," he said, making her look at him eye to eye. "What kind of knife did you take from the kitchen drawer? Think."

"It was like a paring knife, like this long." She indicated about three inches with her shaking fingers.

"It took quite a bit of presence of mind to hide that knife," I said.

"That was good thinking, wasn't it?" A tiny smile crossed her lips.

"Unless you hit him just right in the carotid, a small knife like that probably didn't kill him, then," said Joel, "especially with a coat, jacket or whatever cold weather stuff he was wearing."

My mind did a brief hiccup at Joel's proper identification of a major artery. "But I'll bet he's bleeding some," I said. "You must have stabbed him and run. Good for you. After he grabbed you and took off out of the driveway, how far did he get before he hit the icy patch?"

"Not too far," she said. "Maybe eight blocks. I thought I'd never get back here. I was sliding all over the place. A couple of people passed me in their cars, but nobody stopped to ask if I was okay." Then her eyes narrowed, and she pointed at her shoes, big, black, clunky things. "These are not good for running."

No kidding.

"Rashawna, we're going to get out of here," I said. "I doubt he'll be trying to find you, but we just don't know." I stood up and took control. "Joel, turn on a few lights, and make sure the back door is locked. We'll take Rashawna to my apartment and then go back to the mall."

"What?" said Joel. "We can't do that."

"Oh, yes, we can, and I have a perfectly good reason for going there. Rashawna, I want you to get a clean set of clothes. You can change at my place. Let's go."

We decided to leave Rashawna's car in the hope that, should her wounded abductor come looking for her, he'd have no clue that we'd taken her with us. We wanted him to assume she was still wandering the streets, dazed and confused.

We'd been gone from the mall about forty-five minutes, and by the time we'd dropped Rashawna safely at my apartment, we were back at our survey posts within the hour. This was a huge disappointment to Tara and Brenda, who had gathered twice as many surveys as they would have otherwise.

"You know," said Tara, "we didn't do all these for nothing. What about our bonus?"

"We had a bargain, you know, and we made sure Sybil was clueless," added Brenda.

"It depends on how many surveys you got," I said.

Tara and Brenda ruffled through the surveys on the clipboard. "I got about twelve extras that I guess would be yours," said Brenda.

"I'll give you five dollars for each one of them," I said.

"That would be ..." Brenda's brow scrunched up in a useless attempt to do the math.

"Sixty dollars," said Joel. "Take it or leave it." His scrunched brow was a lot more threatening than Brenda's, and she and Tara both shoved the extra surveys at us and walked off in a huff. I could tell Joel was in no mood to argue. He sighed.

"What's your great plan?" he asked. "How about we hunt this psychopath down, I kill him, and you drive the getaway car?"

"First, I need to know something," I said, ignoring the remark. "Would you recognize Selena's husband if you saw him again?"

"I'm not sure," Joel answered. "I only saw him from a distance that one time he had it out with Selena in the store, and he had that shiner, so he probably looks different now."

"But when she was arrested for domestic violence, he was the one who called it in. If I recall, the news report said she'd been throwing bottles. I wonder if she has even more of a police record. "

"Yeah, I'm telling you that woman is mean, and you should see the mitts on her." He lifted his hands as though they held grapefruits. "Throwing bottles would just be a little light entertainment for her."

"Oh, I've seen the mitts on her, but there's always a reason why people are the way they are, Joel," I said. "We don't know her story." I waved him along with me as I headed for the survey information table. "For now, I think Rashawna will be fine at my place. We'll need to finish out this work day, and then we have some sleuthing to do."

"Aw, come on, Min," whined Joel, "what are you up to?"

I planned to check out the Dollar Store, which I knew would be open for an hour after our survey duties were done. I wanted to do a stakeout of my own. I had a suspicion about Selena's husband, and I hoped we could be around when Selena left work. We might be able to talk to her and get a sense of her relationship with the man. I sketched out my idea for Joel. He looked doubtful, but I promised him we'd check on Rashawna every hour in the meantime.

When we got to the information table, it was swarming with teen girls. Word must have spread. The wigs were a fantastic draw now that noon had passed, and the little darlings were awake, clothed and in full makeup. We approached the table, and I saw Sybil's head bobbing up and down as she stroked the wigs and extolled the virtues of Brilliance shampoo to the eager teens. She saw me.

"Winnie," she shrieked, one hand frantically waving me over. "We need you here." And to Joel, "You too, Joel, sweetie, these girls are dying to answer your survey questions."

For the next four hours Joel and I pounded the mall corridors and gathered the opinions of everyone who looked our way for even two seconds. By suppertime we had sixty more surveys each, and we were feeling pretty good. Reports from Rashawna were also good. She had commandeered the recliner, television and teapot. She'd followed my instructions and changed her clothes, putting the bloodstained ones into a plastic bag. Joel and I promised we'd be back as soon as we could after wrapping up our evening surveys. We didn't tell her of our intended interview with Selena.

At eight o'clock I was beat. Joel didn't look so great himself, and neither of us could stand the idea of doing it all again tomorrow. I tried to think *bonus, bonus,* but even that didn't help. We packed up our supplies and left Sybil finishing up with a few of the other survey workers, including our two cover girls. Tara and Brenda each winked at Joel as we headed for the Dollar Store.

The mall was much quieter now. The store was nearly empty when we walked in. Only one checkout was open, and Selena was nowhere in sight.

"Was Selena supposed to work tonight?" I asked Joel.

"Yeah, she works most weekends," he said. He nodded to the clerk at the one checkout and began to walk toward the back of the store. "Hey, Cheryl, Selena around?" he called over his shoulder to the girl.

"Hi, Joel," she said. "Yeah, she worked for a couple hours this afternoon, then she took off. Said her husband was sick. She asked me to cover the rest of her shift." Cheryl turned her attention to what appeared to be the last customer of the day. "I had a date, too, but at least it's overtime," she added in an aside to me.

"When you're done, could I ask you a couple of questions?"

"Yeah, sure. I have to hang around until nine," she answered. "That'll be six forty-eight," she said to the customer.

Joel had disappeared somewhere among the aisles, and I watched as Cheryl bagged the customer's items. I was eager to ask her about Selena's character and whether she'd confided in Cheryl.

"Okay, shoot," said Cheryl. She leaned against the counter and glanced at her watch.

"You took Selena's shift tonight, so I assume she's a friend?"

"Well, as much as anybody could be a friend to her. She's got some serious issues," said Cheryl.

"Really? Like what?"

"She told me once that her stepfather beat her mom all the time and snuck into Selena's bedroom a couple of times, you know, trying to get into her bed, if you get my drift."

"Oh, yeah," I said, "I get it. Poor girl."

"Selena's a tough cookie, though. The guy never got anywhere, at least that she told me about. Guess her dad left after the mother started seeing this other guy. She adored her Pop. That's what she called him, Pop."

I was beginning to get a clearer picture of Selena and felt some sympathy for her.

"One more thing," said Cheryl. "The family moved up here from downstate when Selena was only thirteen. She had a real tough time with that."

"Do you know where she went to high school?" I asked.

"Nope," said Cheryl with another glance at her watch. She rubbed her neck and yawned. "I don't know a whole lot more about her. She's not the easiest person to talk to. Keeps to herself a lot."

We both turned toward the back of the store when we heard a big thud. "Excuse me," I said and went to find Joel.

He must have heard the thud, too. I found him in paper towels and napkins at the back of the store. He put his finger to his lips as I approached and pointed at the tile floor just outside the employee's only door. There on the speckled tile was a rust-colored smear. Blood? Very interesting. Joel pushed the door open soundlessly, and we stepped into a small room. Metal floor-to-ceiling storage shelves ran the length of the back wall. To our left sat one of those cheap, white, plastic picnic tables surrounded by some plastic chairs. On the opposite wall there was a counter with a sink, a coffeemaker and one overhead cupboard. Beside the counter sat a full-size refrigerator with the same colored blotches on the handle that we'd seen on the floor. We walked toward the refrigerator, and there was a sudden gush of air as the back door, partially obscured by the metal shelves, burst open.

Joel dodged the shelves and took off yelling. "Selena!"

I scurried after him and got outside just in time to see Selena and a man jump into a blue pickup truck and slam the doors. Selena's arms were loaded with packages. She shoved them through the truck door, jumped into the driver's seat, turned the engine over and gunned it. Joel almost made it to the truck door, but Selena slammed her foot down and tore out of the parking lot, causing him to miss the door handle by inches. Joel began running but soon gave up. He headed back to me slamming the air with his fists.

"Gaahhh!" he screamed.

"Joel," I called to him, "did you see the plate number?"

"The plate! No, I was only thinking of that guy with her."

"Minnie?" A deep voice came from behind me. I turned and saw Dan Horowitz.

"Oh, Dan," I said, hugely relieved. "I'm so glad you came."

Joel reached my side. "What's going on?" he asked, trying to control his rage. He glanced back into the parking lot and pounded the air again.

"I called Dan on our last break and told him what's been going on today, Joel," I said. "I had a hunch about Selena's husband, and I wanted to put Dan on the alert."

"Thanks for the heads up to meet you here this evening. I've called for backup. We'll be going over the employees' lounge when they get here," said Dan. "I'll have a few officers checking out the blood, taking photos and collecting other evidence. Where's your other friend?"

"Rashawna?" I asked.

"Is that her name? She's the one who says she was abducted this morning?"

"She's at my apartment right now," I said. I'd filled Dan in on Rashawna's terrifying morning when I'd called him earlier.

Dan raised one eyebrow at me before he went on. "Any reason why we haven't heard from her yet?" he asked.

"Um, well," I stammered, "when she finally got back to her house she was really shaken up. She's very nervous about the whole thing." I didn't know what else to say to him and was relieved when he spoke.

"We'd like her to fill out a police report, if she's sufficiently over her fright, that is," Dan said.

"Could it wait until morning?" asked Joel. "She's had an awful day. We can get her down there before we come to work in the morning."

"You guys have to work tomorrow too, huh?"

"It's a special survey blitz for a new shampoo," I said.

"Ah, I wondered what those wig tables were for. Anyway, my team should be done here in a half hour or so," said Dan. "We'll need to question you and ..." Dan threw Joel a questioning look.

"Joel," said Joel and put out his hand.

"Joel. Have I heard of you from Sergeant Hobart maybe?"

Palms up, Joel quickly interrupted him. "Minnie, we'd better get back to Rashawna." He took my arm and tried to steer me back into the mall.

I smiled. "We'll have to give our own report first, Joel," I said. "Can you take it, Dan, or should we talk to someone else?"

"Come on," said Dan, still looking with interest at Joel. We followed Dan back through the lounge where yellow tape covered the doorways and lay across the refrigerator. We went back into the mall, sat on a bench and told him what we'd seen. We tried to give him some idea of the man Selena was with. Unfortunately, we hadn't seen his face, so we weren't much help there. The whole thing took about fifteen minutes, and Joel was like a bee in a tar bucket from wanting to get back to Rashawna.

"We've done about what we can do tonight," said Dan finally. "I've got a BOLO out for a blue pickup truck with the plate number you gave me. I'll let you know if we round them up."

"BOLO," said Joel. "I've heard that word."

"It's an acronym for 'be on the lookout'," said Dan.

"Good, that's good," said Joel, sighing. Suddenly the starch had gone all out of him, and I understood. I was weary to the bone myself.

"Let's go," I said.

I knocked on my own apartment door to let Rashawna know it was Joel and me. She let us in and hugged us. The air wafting in from the kitchen smelled strangely sweet.

"I made Snickerdoodles," said Rashawna, as she noticed me looking around and sniffing. "I hope you don't mind, Minnie. I peeked through your cupboards, and you had all the ingredients. My grandma Jones used to make them all the time, and after the day I just had I needed to do something."

"Rashawna," I said gently, "it's okay. I'm sure you were going nuts here waiting for us. They smell wonderful."

Joel and I took off our coats and collapsed in the living room. Rashawna put the teapot on, and ten minutes later we had hot tea and cookies before us. In spite of the horrors of the day — one being no lunch and two, no dinner — it felt quite cozy.

"We've got good news and bad news," I said.

"Oh, great," said Rashawna, shrinking into the back of the sofa, "you found out that guy I stabbed died?"

"No, the last time we saw him he was quite alive," I said.

Rashawna's eyes nearly popped out of her head. "You *saw* him?"

"Not exactly. We saw somebody, and we think he's Selena's husband," said Joel between cookie bites. He curled up on the sofa next to her.

"No wacky way," said Rashawna.

"We nearly had Selena and this guy cornered in the employees' lounge at the Dollar Store," said Joel, "but they were too fast for us, slipped right out the back of the store."

"They got away in a blue pickup truck just before the police got there," I said. My eyes glazed over briefly. The cookies were almost as good as Taffy Tails.

"Wow, who called the cops?" asked Rashawna. Her voice was small and quiet.

"What's the matter, honey?" I asked.

"Did you tell them I was the one who stabbed him?"

"We kind of left that out of the conversation," answered Joel, "but we have to take you in tomorrow morning."

"TAKE ME IN?" Now she was ramrod straight on the couch.

"They just want you down at the station to fill out a police report," said Joel quickly. "I guess I shouldn't have said 'take you in,' but going in to do a police report is a lot different than being called in for questioning, if that's what you were thinking." He put his arm around her shoulder.

"What questions? I don't want to answer any questions. And how do you know about going in for questioning?" She pulled back from Joel and glared at him.

"Rashawna, calm down," I said. "We'll be right there with you. You were the one who was attacked. You don't have anything to be worried about. All you have to do is answer the questions on a form and show some identification."

"Well ..."

"I should have insisted on getting you in there to give a report right away, but I guess I got carried away with my idea about Selena's husband. I'm nearly certain he's the one who's been harassing us."

"But why?" cried Rashawna.

"We haven't quite figured that out yet," I said. "Let's take care of the report first."

"Actually, Min, I have something to do in the morning," said Joel. "You two will have to go in without me." He seemed resolute.

"What do you have to do so early in the morning?" I asked. "We have to be at the mall at eight, you know."

"Yup, I know, and I'll be there, but I can't go to the police station."

I knew there was no way to force him to go with us. Joel was a man of mystery, and I was beginning to wonder if we should know a little, or maybe a lot, more about him. If he hadn't stuck by us through this whole scary mess, my suspicious character radar would have been somewhere near the moon.

Rashawna jumped up from the couch. "What'll I wear?" she wailed.

Looking at her face, I didn't know whether to laugh or cry. We each handle a crisis in our own way, and I gave her the benefit of the doubt when Rashawna turned her upcoming appearance at the police station into a wardrobe dilemma. Joel wasn't quite getting that, though.

"You women," he snapped. "It's not a fancy ball. It doesn't matter what you wear."

Rashawna flopped back down beside him. "I know," she said, "I'm just scared."

I heard music — Beethoven, to be exact. My cell was chiming away in my purse. Who in the world could that be? I heaved out of my recliner and found my handbag. "Hang on," I said to the impatient caller. I looked at the caller ID and then remembered I'd given Dan my new cell number.

"Minnie?" he said. "I hope you're not annoyed that I'm calling, but I forgot to tell you something when I saw you tonight."

"No problem, Dan, we're still up," I said. "What have you got?"

"Well, this will be on the television news tonight, but I'll tell you ahead of the report. The name of the man they found dead in the Hannaford parking lot a few nights ago is Roberto Rodriguez. He was wearing a yellow, hooded sweatshirt and had a strange forehead. Kind of scrunchy was the way they described it. Ring any bells?" Dan asked.

My mind was a blank in the manner of a horror movie zombie. Too much had happened today for me to make any connections. Nothing came to mind. "Not at the moment," I said, "but thank you so much for letting me know." I jotted the name down on the grocery list pad I kept on the kitchen counter.

Dan filled me in on a few other tidbits from the employee lounge investigation and reminded me about encouraging Rashawna to go to the station in the morning.

"No problem," I said and rang off.

Joel and Rashawna had bored holes through my back the whole time I was on the phone and wanted to know about the call the instant it ended.

"Well, for once we won't have to count on the evening news for important information," I said.

"Yeah, especially those last few words which are all we ever get," said Rashawna.

"The man found dead in the grocery parking lot the other night was Roberto Rodriguez. One EMT mentioned his forehead. He had three big cysts just over his eyebrows that made him look kind of deformed. The name doesn't mean a thing to me." I gave them a questioning look.

"Oh, my gosh, Minnie," said Rashawna. Big cat food saucer eyes stared at me.

"What? Do you know him?"

She looked at Joel, who was running his hands through his hair. "Minnie, that guy has the same last name as Selena's husband."

Seventeen

"That could just be a coincidence," I said, and a darned scary one, too. My mind was reeling, and it was too late in the day for reeling. I sat down and took a long pull on my tea. I grabbed another Snickerdoodle.

"Could just be a big ol' scary coincidence," said Joel, echoing my thoughts.

"Yeah, what you said," said Rashawna.

"Or not," I said. "Are we too tired and worn out to think about this?" I asked.

"I am," said Joel.

"Me, too," said Rashawna. "Minnie, am I staying here tonight?"

"Yes, you are, and Joel," I said, turning to him, "if you'd like, you can have the chair-bed. Rashawna, you're in with me. My bed's a queen size, so there's lots of room. Okay?"

"I've got somewhere to stay tonight, Min, but thanks," said Joel.

"You want us to take you somewhere?" asked Rashawna.

By us, she meant me.

"No, I'm good," he said, snagging his cell from the pants pocket down by his knee. "I'll call a buddy to come get me."

I was in no mood to have anything but peace, and it must have shown on my face. It was nearly ten-thirty, and any more conversation on anything would have been extremely unproductive. I suggested an early night and got no argument. Joel put on his coat, opened the door with one hand and punched his cell with the other. He lifted his chin by way of saying goodbye and was gone.

I was up first the next morning. It was six o'clock. I hit the shower and shrugged into my robe, then went to start breakfast. No sense facing whatever this day would bring with an empty stomach. I cracked some eggs into a bowl and whisked in a little milk. I poured them into a pan and turned the heat on low. When the teakettle whistled, Rashawna popped her head up from the chair-bed and smiled. Then it hit what day it was, and she lurched out of the covers. "What time is it?"

"We have plenty of time," I said cheerily, not feeling it. "I've got scrambled eggs and scones for breakfast."

Rashawna's shoulders slumped, and she wrapped herself in the flannel sheet from her bed. Her curls were a little flat, and her eyes were bloodshot. "I just had the most awful, sudden thought," she said. "I have to wear my clothes from yesterday. I only brought one outfit over from my house when we ran out of there."

Oh, the heartaches of youth. I sighed. "Tell you what," I said. "Go right now and take your shower. When you're done, hang your pants and shirt in the steamy bathroom, and they'll look as good as new when you're done with breakfast and ready to put them back on."

She brightened considerably at that. "Good idea, Min. I washed out my dainties last night and hung them over the curtain rod, so I'm all set."

Did I dare hazard a peek at my curtain rod? Nah, didn't want to burn the eggs. "Go," I said, pointing down the hall to the bathroom. "We don't have all that much time."

She stumbled up from the chair-bed and retrieved her shirt and pants from the floor. The flannel sheet wrapped all around her forced her to take little geisha-like steps all the way to the bathroom. "I'll be out in a few," she said. "Eggs smell yummy!"

I poured hot water into the teapot and took a package of blueberry scones from the freezer. I took out two and put two back. These would only take a few minutes to heat in the microwave. I put plates, forks, knives and napkins on the table, and then I poured some orange juice into pretty glasses. The bathroom door snicked open.

"Wow," said Rashawna, "this looks great."

She came up behind me wrapped in two towels, one on her head and one around her torso. I guess we were going for the spa look this morning. I scooped some eggs onto her plate and retrieved the scones from the oven. I put one on each of our plates and set strawberry jam in the middle of the table.

"I've been thinking about something, Minnie," said Rashawna.

"Shoot," I said, as I tipped the pan for the rest of the eggs to slide onto my plate.

"Did you ever notice how Joel never called me by my name until yesterday? He always said Babe or Curly but never Rashawna."

I mulled it over while my first sip of tea went down. She was right. "What do you think that means?" I asked.

"I don't know," she said, "maybe he was saving something back. Maybe calling me by my name was too intimate, you know, until now."

Another bit of insight from this enigmatic young woman. "He was very frightened for you, Rashawna," I said. "Yesterday was not fun and games. I think he cares quite a bit about what happens to you."

Rashawna's cell interrupted our conversation, and I got a flash of bare leg and rear end as she bolted up to answer it. "Hi," she said, ducking her head into the phone. "Yeah, we're just finishing up breakfast, and then we're leaving." As she spoke her face telegraphed her returning anxiety about her trip downtown. Of course she was talking to Joel. She hung up and came back to the table. "That was Joel. He says he'll be about ten minutes late this morning for the survey job, but he'll be there."

I stood and began clearing the table. "Okay, we've got to get moving," I said. "You get dressed and do your thing in the bathroom, and I'll clean up here."

Rashawna got up and went to the big living room window, where she swooped her hand to the top of the curtain rod and pulled down her peach colored panties and bra. "Be right out," she said. There was a quaver in her voice.

Poor kid. My heart went out to her, and I hoped she'd be okay with me leaving her at the police station for however long it took to give her report. I'd arranged with Dan for someone to drive Rashawna over to the mall when she was done. I finished up in the kitchen and went to get dressed.

We pulled up in front of the police station at seven forty-five. Rashawna had been quietly trembling beside me during the entire drive over. She got out of the car and took the steps in front of the station slowly. It was making me nuts, and with great effort I held back the urge to grab her elbow and march her along. I didn't want to leave her, and I didn't want to be late to the mall, and I didn't want to be middleaged and fat, either, but there we were.

Sam Hobart smiled at us when we finally got inside, and I told him why we were there.

"Oh, yes," said Sam. "I remember you both from a few nights ago. I'll let someone know you're here." He motioned Rashawna and me to a long bench along the opposite wall and disappeared down the hall. Rashawna looked small and scared sitting there. I had to act. I took her hand and sat down beside her, me being the kindly spider and all.

"Rashawna, I want you to do something for me," I said. "Look at me, and listen."

She looked at me, and there were tears gathering at the edges of her eyes. "I want you to think of your Aunt Lucretia," I said.

"Aunt Lucretia?" She blinked.

"I don't know much about her, but it seems to me that if she was in this situation, she'd use her will and her faith to guide her."

She swiped the back of her hand over her eyes and smiled. "You're right, Minnie, I guess she would." Her toes tapped lightly on the tile floor.

"I think deep down you're strong like her and like your Grandma Jones, too. I want you to think of that when you give this report. You haven't done anything wrong," I said, repeating myself from the night before. "You may end up being a useful witness in a very tangled case, and you should try to stay focused and helpful. You're not a scared little rabbit. You're Rashawna Jones, and the women you come from are brave and resourceful."

Rashawna sat tall and looked around. "Well, I guess this place isn't going to get to me," she said. Her voice came stronger. "I think I'll be okay."

I could tell a little of her snappy was coming back. A bit of light was in her eyes.

"Grandma Jones, I'll think of her."

I hoped my words had the desired effect and didn't have her thinking she could spit-hex anything here at the station. I sighed and stood up. "I know you will," I said. "I've asked for someone to drop you at the mall when you're done. Joel and I will be waiting for you." I reached over and gave her a hug and then turned to go. I looked up and saw a policewoman coming down the hall.

"Miss Jones?" the officer said, looking at Rashawna.

"Yes, that's me," said Rashawna. She stood up and smoothed her pants, then followed the woman with her head high and curls bouncing.

I was so proud.

I hurried back to my car. I had about seven minutes to get to the mall, but I knew I could make it in four. As I drove I tried to wrap my mind around the tangled mess this case had become. I just knew we'd get it figured out. I was scary-excited, and all my Agatha reading was buzzing around in my head. Methodical and clear thinking came to my aid. Were the mall stalker and Selena's husband related, brothers or cousins, maybe? Had one killed the other? And what was with the blue truck, and where the heck was Joel? Most importantly, what did any of this have to do with the red shoelace killer? The mall came into view just as my head was about to explode from thinking about all of it. I sent up a quick prayer that Rashawna would be okay, and then I set my mind to survey taking. I would be a real dynamo today.

Sybil hailed me as soon as she saw me hustling toward her. "Winnie! Over here!"

As if I would go anywhere else. "I'm not Winnie, but I could go look for her, I guess," I said when I got near enough for Sybil to hear me. I had some brave in me, too.

"You're not?" she said, looking puzzled. "Didn't you work for me yesterday?"

I sighed. "Yes, Miss Grant, I did, but my name is Minnie with an M, not Winnie." I offered her a tiny smile so she wouldn't take too great offense.

"Oh, my goodness, I am so sorry, Minnie. Do you know how many people I work with on these things? I'm lucky I can get my own name right."

Did I say this lady was good? She knew just what to say to someone who was going to be hustling mall shoppers for the next ten hours.

"It's okay, and I do understand. Anyway, what's up?"

"I've just been checking my list of workers, and I seem to be missing one," she said.

Uh oh. I was afraid this would happen. Rashawna hadn't shown up at all yesterday, and Joel would be late today. "One of my co-workers, Rashawna Jones, was not feeling well yesterday. I know, I spoke with her," I said. "Unfortunately, she'll be a little late today, and so will Joel."

"Oh, I'm not too worried about Joel," said Sybil. "He's such a fast worker, he can get twice the surveys in half the time. But this Jones person, what do you know about her?"

"I've worked with her for quite a while. In fact, she's the one who recruited Joel," I said. "She's very good at what she does."

Sybil frowned.

"Rashawna made some comments about shiny hair at the orientation on Friday. You told her she could be a real star. Do you remember that?" I asked.

"Sort of," she said and began checking off boxes on some kind of spreadsheet she had on her clipboard. "Anyway, could you tell anyone you see who's working for us to just keep on doing what they did yesterday, only faster? I really want to wrap this up by eight tonight."

"Sure, "I said. "Anybody who comes to this station will get the *go get 'em* from me." I made a rah-rah sign with my balled fists and grinned.

"You're a lifesaver Win-, uh, Minnie," said Sybil. She patted my arm and glanced down the mall corridor. "I'll be at the other end." And off she went.

The table had been set up again, and the few people who were in the mall at that early hour didn't look very interested. I sat in the chair behind the table and rifled through the box full of clipboards. I didn't suppose it mattered which ones I took, so I grabbed three in anticipation of Joel and Rashawna turning up soon. I threw an eye at the mall again, and then I spotted her, the black-eyed blonde. She had that new shoe store, All in Red, in her sights, strolling towards it as she blew at the foam on a fresh cup of coffee. I looked around. Still not much action in the mall. I got up and made tracks for the shoe store.

As I entered I was a little overwhelmed by the new smell of it. From the customer seating to the shiny glass and chrome-like display shelving, everything snapped and crackled with newness. The blonde was behind the counter, opening her cash drawer. Clouds of wonderful-smelling mocha latte, with maybe a hint of cinnamon, rose in the air around her. She looked up when I approached.

"Can I help you?"

"I hope so," I said. "I have a friend you've spoken to about a man who's been kind of stalking the mall. She and I do surveys together."

"I know who you mean, and I know your friend," said the blonde, waving a hand at me. She reached into a drawer behind the counter and took out a name badge. It read Gretchen. Good, now I had a name. She fiddled with the badge to position it just right on her shirt.

"And that guy?" Gretchen continued, "He's real scary. It's like his forehead can't straighten out." She made her own forehead scrunch up by way of demonstration. I could see why she and Rashawna hit it off. My stomach did a little flip-flop at the realization that she was describing one of the mall stalker's distinguishing features, one exhibited by Roberto Rodriguez.

"Anyway," I said, "I was told that he'd come in here asking about red shoes."

"Yeah, everybody does," said Gretchen motioning to the walls, which were covered with red everything, and giving me a *duh* look. "But he wanted to know about these babies." She reached back and pulled a pair of pale gray, high-topped sneakers out of a display and plopped them on the counter in front of me. The laces were at least forty inches long and blood red.

"Uh, but he didn't buy them, right?" I asked.

"No, but he kept touching the laces and asking me about anybody else who might have wanted them. He didn't look like he could afford them at two hundred and forty bucks a pop. The next day someone bought a pair, but the weird guy was gone by then, and I mean gone. Haven't seen him prowling around since."

I looked at the shoes. Two forty? Wow, was I out of touch with the fashion world or what? "Was it a man or woman who bought them?" I asked, suddenly thinking of Selena.

"Oh, it was a woman, real pretty, too, but not nice. Nope, not nice at all," said Gretchen. She picked up her latte and blew, sipped and looked past me at the customer who had come in behind me. Her smile dismissed me, and she walked out to greet her potential customer.

I thanked Gretchen for the information as I passed her and her prey and left the store. I picked up speed as I got nearer our survey table. Rashawna stood there, running her fingers through the red wig. She smiled when she saw me.

Eighteen

"It was a breeze, Minnie," said Rashawna, beaming. "I just did like you said and let my true side come out, you know, the brave, resourceful woman."

"Well, good for you, Rashawna," I said, beaming back at her. "We have a break at ten, and you can tell me all about it then. Here's your clipboard and some survey forms." I handed them over to her and noticed her look of disappointment. "I really do want to hear about it, honey, but we've got to get these surveys done. Sybil's in a tizzy." I hoped she wasn't going to let the moment drag. "Your Aunt Lucretia and Grandma Jones would be as proud of you as I am," I added gently. "Let's do what we do best."

"I'm all about it," said Rashawna. She took the clipboard from me and stashed her purse and jacket under the table, then took up her post at the bottom of the elevator. She hadn't even asked me where Joel was.

I wasn't going to take much time worrying about it either, and I got to the business of racking up surveys. Sybil came by our table an hour later and did a count. We had thirty more for her between Rashawna and me. When Sybil asked about Joel, I told her I wasn't sure if he was at another station or not. Her cell phone rang, and she answered it as she sped off to another location. I watched as her hands did some of the communicating, unseen by the caller, of course.

A few minutes before ten Rashawna came back to the table with fifteen more surveys. "So where the heck is Joel?" she asked.

"I don't know," I said, "but he'll show up at the most unexpected time, count on it."

"I could use a hot cup of Joe," said Rashawna. "You?"

"Yup, let's take our break."

We only had fifteen minutes, but we got our coffees quickly and found a quiet corner to enjoy them. The mall still wasn't very full, which always seemed to be the case on Sunday mornings. By two o'clock, though, the younger crowd should have recovered from their Saturday night fun and would be back here for more. Girls and women under forty were our prime targets, and I hoped they all wanted to do some early holiday shopping. We had a bonus at stake here, after all.

Rashawna took a tentative sip of her steaming coffee, leaned back in her seat and heaved a huge sigh. "I am so glad that's over."

"I assume you're speaking of the police report. So how was it?" I asked. "You weren't there very long."

"They put me in a small room with a couple of other people, and then that nice woman who came to get me asked me what happened. She wrote it all down and asked to see my driver's license for identification. That was it."

"Did you tell them about the knife?"

"Uh, well, no," she said.

"Rashawna," I growled.

"I just couldn't, Minnie." Another slurp of coffee. "That detective was real nice, and I gave her my name, address, all that stuff, and then she asked a couple of questions to get me started. So I told her how I was waiting for my plow guy and all of that, and even said about the teabag, but I couldn't tell her about the knife." She grabbed her stomach.

"It's okay," I said. "I guess that's all you can do for now, and you can always add to the report later if you want to. Besides, it's up to him to file a report against *you* if he wants to report it, and I'll bet he doesn't want to do that."

"You think he would?"

"No, I don't."

"I mean, he could say I jumped in his truck and attacked him or something."

"Don't even worry about it. If he's who we think he is, he's not going to do that," I said.

"We means you and Joel, right?"

"Right," I said. "Here's the thing. Joel and I don't know if Selena's husband is the same guy who grabbed you because we're not sure what dear hubby looks like. Joel saw him with Selena once and from a distance, plus the guy had a black eye. And he and Selena were already out the door last night when Joel and I were in the employees' lounge at the Dollar Store, so we didn't get a good look at him then, either." I took another sip of my coffee and peeked at my watch.

"So, if the guy who took me," said Rashawna, "is the same guy who's married to Selena, then I'm the only one of the three of us who's seen his face." She took the top off of her coffee cup and blew briskly. "How are we gonna know for sure?"

"You said you could identify him if you saw him again, right?"

"I'm pretty sure I could, but Minnie, I was so scared."

I patted her arm. "I know, I know, but we've done what we could, and we have to let the police do their job. Maybe they found the guy, and we just don't know it yet. We'd better head back to work. Sybil will be prowling for more surveys soon." I wasn't even going to mention identifying anyone in a lineup.

Two hours and forty surveys later, we came up for air. Rashawna had done a wide swath on both sides of the escalator and had hauled in twenty-five more surveys. She was loving the beauty and grooming angle of this project, and the people she talked with knew it. They had responded with great enthusiasm. She'd sent them all to me for wig stroking, coupons and sample shampoo bottles when they'd finished the survey.

"I'm starving, and I'm worried," said Rashawna, returning to the information table.

"I don't know where he is," I said, knowing her thoughts.

"I've sneaked two calls to his cell so far, but he's not answering," said Rashawna.

"I've only sneaked one," I said. Just then, over her right shoulder, I saw someone coming around the right side of the escalator at high speed. It was Joel. He came up swiftly behind Rashawna and slid his arm around her waist.

"You're looking so good, Curly," he said.

She swung her head around, whapping him in the face with her curls. "Where've you been?"

Joel pulled a long, dark hair off his lip. "You two ready for lunch? I've got some news."

"Are you gonna answer me?" Rashawna had her angry up and wasn't budging.

"Okay, okay," said Joel. "I was on a mini-stakeout."

"What?" Rashawna and I said at the same time.

"Come on," said Joel. He led us into the food court, and we ordered shrimp egg rolls, rice and sodas at the Best of China counter. We sat.

"I just can't wait to hear about your mini-stakeout, Joel," I said. Boy, that egg roll was hot. I decided to let it sit for a minute.

"Well, I've been trying to figure out the blue truck angle," said Joel, chomping the egg roll and gasping a little. He fisted his chest and took a swig of soda. "Whoa, man, egg roll from hell." Another swig. "Gotta love that Best of China."

"You went a little heavy on that spicy mustard. Duh!" said Rashawna.

Joel coughed again and continued. "Anyway, remember when I talked to the waitress at the fish place? She said she'd seen the truck, and it reminded her of one her old boyfriend had."

"Makes me wonder if there's a Blue Trucks 'R' Us dealer around here," said Rashawna. She forked some rice into her mouth.

Joel smiled. "I borrowed a car from my buddy, the one I stayed with last night, and went over to Mack's."

"After the day we had yesterday, you went on another stakeout?" I said, incredulous.

"When I get a bug up my ..." Joel stopped and coughed. "Uh, sorry, when I'm really curious about something I gotta find out as much as I can."

"So, what happened?" asked Rashawna.

"Well, before the stakeout part I went inside to look around and see if that waitress was there."

"Was she?" I asked.

"Yeah, and what did she look like?"

Guess who asked that?

"Okay, you two just let me tell the story. I won't leave anything out." Joel put his fork down and looked pointedly at us.

"You're right," I said. "We'll be quiet and eat, and you tell us what happened." Besides, my egg roll had cooled a bit and smelled wonderful.

"The waitress wasn't there, but the cook was. He must be the only one they have. Anyway, there was a guy picking up an order ahead of me, so I just looked around, kind of getting my bearings and, well, calming myself."

"Nothing like calm for getting the job done," I said then covered my mouth. "Sorry," I whispered.

"My idea was to order some food and then ask the guy about his cousin and the truck. So I'm giving him my order, and I notice he looks, real quick like, over my shoulder. When I turn around to see what he's looking at, I see taillights at the side of the building like someone's pulling into the driveway out there. He tells me it'll be ten minutes, and then he goes through the kitchen and into the back room." Joel scraped the last bits of rice from his paper plate and finished his soda. He jiggled the ice in his soda cup. "I heard the back door open and then some loud voices. Funny, one of them sounded just like Selena." He smacked the cup down on the table. "And she didn't sound happy."

"No wacky way!" shrieked Rashawna. She looked around quickly and ducked her head. "What the heck were they doing there?" she whispered.

"That's what I wanted to know," said Joel. "I slunk to the other side of the counter so I could look into the back room. It was Selena, all right. She was helping someone up the back stairs. I didn't even know that place had an upstairs."

"Actually, I think the fry cook lives upstairs," I said. "When Dan and I were there I heard some kids call him Eddie. I did a Google search on Mack's Pier and found a link to an article from several years ago. Eddie's dad Sal owned the place before he did, from back in the '70s. After the old man died, Eddie took over. That was about eight years ago."

"Interesting," said Joel, nodding. "Anyway, Eddie came back into the kitchen right away, and I turned around quick so he wouldn't notice I'd been watching. I had my order in about ten minutes." Joel looked very satisfied with his report.

"Where does the stakeout part come in?" I asked.

"I'm getting to that," said Joel. "A couple more people came in while I was chowing my fish, and I watched that Eddie with an eagle eye. One thing I noticed when he came out to take an order at a table. He's got huge feet." Joel held out fish-story hands to about fourteen inches.

"Oh!" Rashawna's hand shot across the table, and she tugged Joel's sleeve. "That stalker guy? He had huge feet, too."

"And we think he's the one that got killed in the Hannaford parking lot," I said. "Good grief, I wonder if they're all related to each other."

"That's just too weird," said Joel. "After that I left and sat for a while in my buddy's car, you know, across the street so nobody would notice me."

"Anything happen?" I asked.

"Nope, it was quiet as a graveyard after the last customer left. Eddie killed the lights in the place, and that was it."

"So where were you this morning?" asked Rashawna. Her egg roll had one bite out of it.

"Hang on, there's more," said Joel, eyeing her plate. "I decided to find out the plate number on the truck parked on the side of the building. My heart was here," he indicated his throat, "but I got across the street okay, and then I saw the back of the truck was covered with a tarp. It was dark, but I have one of those miniature flashlights on my key ring, and I lifted the tarp and could just make out the number."

"Ah," said Rashawna, "was it Orange Tea Bag 843?"

"Bingo, baby," said Joel, gently punching her arm. "It was kind of a rush to know for sure. Then I decided to look through the truck windows, in case there was anything else, like maybe your smashed cell." Joel looked at Rashawna for some sign of approval.

"If I'd known I would have been so scared for you," said Rashawna, fawning.

"I didn't see a smashed cell phone, that truck floor was really dark and dirty, but I did see one thing: a newspaper on the seat. It looked like that story we saw the other day on the Red Shoelace ..."

"Killer!" blurted Rashawna. "I could smack myself." She did so. "I saw that same paper sitting on the seat when I was in that truck. It just came to me now like a vision."

"Or sudden recall," I said. "Now that you're out of immediate danger, you're able to recall your abduction more clearly, grasping small details like the newspaper."

Gosh, the pseudo behavioral scientist in me was just busting right out.

"I'll bet that's it," gushed Rashawna, "and you know, I think one of those girls in the funeral picture was marked."

"Marked?"

Rashawna put her fingertips to her forehead and closed her eyes. "I'm seeing a circle or an X," she said.

Oh, brother. "If one of them was marked in some way that could mean the killer's ready to strike again. There's a good possibility he has it in for all three friends," I said. "Was there anything else?" I asked, turning to Joel.

"I didn't look too long after that. I heard a noise in the alley, and I gotta tell ya, I was shaking like dice in a Yahtzee cup by the time I got outta there." He cranked his neck back and forth and sighed.

"You did a great job, Joel," I said. "What you two have found out really advances our theory of a possible vendetta from the killer's high school days."

"Wow," said Joel, whistling, "a vendetta. There's a whole bunch of old movies about that right there."

"Did it cross your mind to call the police?" I asked.

"I was so hyped about getting all this good info for our case, I guess it slipped my mind."

"So why were you late this morning?" Rashawna asked, her sudden recall kicking in again. Curiously, she was more interested in that than the exciting discovery we'd just made.

"Getting my car back," said Joel, grinning. "I finally got caught up on my insurance payments, and I have wheels again." He seemed relieved to have the subject changed.

"Oh, honey, that's wonderful," said Rashawna. Her delight was soon interrupted.

"Joel!"

Two giggly, female voices blared across the food court. The three of us looked up to see Tara and Brenda as they came waving and swaying towards us.

"Oh, I really need this right now," said Joel, averting his eyes from Rashawna.

Brenda got to the table first. She slapped a pile of papers down. "Forty-five, count 'em," she said triumphantly.

Tara laid a smaller pile down. "Thirty," she said, favoring Joel with a dazzling smile.

"Heh, heh, thanks ladies," said Joel. "You have no idea what you've done for us here." He stood up quickly, straightened his shoulders and faced the table. He smiled at Rashawna. "Tara, Brenda, I'd like you to meet my girlfriend, Rashawna Jones."

For the remainder of the afternoon Rashawna acted like a queen on a lace and satin pillow. I had to hand it to Joel, he'd pulled himself out of one hot chili pot at the end of our lunch hour. Rashawna's face had gone from gathering fury to utter delight when Joel pronounced that one word, *girlfriend*. It was amazing. The gist of that brief episode was this: Joel had cut the same deal with Brenda and Tara as he and I had the day before. He had the two of them hustling surveys for part, or maybe all, at that point, of his bonus. No wonder Sybil called him a charmer. I had to admire his sheer boldness.

At five o'clock Sybil gathered all the survey workers at the primary set-up table. She looked beat, but she had good news. We only had about sixty more surveys to get to make our goal. We had three hours left to work, but she promised we could all leave the instant survey number sixty hit the pile. We had a dinner break coming up, but most of us decided not to take it. The chance to leave early paled next to the prospect of another Roaring Gate food court supper. Having met our goal meant bonuses, too. It was a pretty happy bunch that set out to finish up the job.

Nineteen

At six-thirty Joel, Rashawna and I were standing outside the mall in the frigid air trying to decide where to have supper. Joel himself had brought in survey number sixty, and it was time to celebrate. After all, we had bonus money coming.

"I just heard about a rib place that's supposed to be pretty good," I said. "It's not too expensive, and we could be there in about fifteen minutes."

"Sounds good to me," said Joel. "'Course, I might need a small loan from you ladies until payday." He coughed and ducked his head.

"No problem," said Rashawna, her voice dripping honey. She was quite obviously still in the thrall of his recent declaration regarding her girlfriend status in his life.

"Where is this place, Minnie?" asked Joel.

"It's out past the new theater complex, and actually we have to go right by Mack's Pier to get there." I paused for effect, and it had a great one on Rashawna.

"I will be crouched low when we hit that stretch of highway," she said.

"It would be kind of interesting to see if that blue truck is still there," said Joel. He glanced at Rashawna and held both hands up, palms out, as she glared back at him. "Or not."

"Tell you what," I said, "we'll go to the rib place first and have a good supper. Everything else is on hold, including Mack's. Deal?"

"Deal," said Rashawna, relaxing a little.

"Joel, we can go in my car, and I'll drop you back here to get yours when we're done."

"Sounds good, Min."

"Aw, I was kind of hoping to see your wheels, Joel," whined Rashawna.

"You will, honey, you will. For now let's get going. My stomach's thinking my throat's been slit."

Rashawna winced.

"It's just a little joke. Come on. Where's your car, Min?"

"Lot H," I said, "where it always is." We walked past the light pools in the parking lot toward the big pole with the H on it. There weren't a lot of cars around; the weekend was really dying down. The moviegoers would be ready to hit the mall theaters in about an hour, but the shoppers had given up for the day.

"How'd you hear about this rib place, Minnie?" asked Rashawna.

"There's a bulletin board in the laundry room at my apartment complex, and I saw a flyer for it. My buddy Briscoe also recommended it."

"You have a buddy named Briscoe?" asked Joel. His eyebrows were near his hairline, and he fought the urge to laugh.

"It's an old family name, Southern, I think. He's a little quirky but harmless," I said. "Anyway, I hope the place is good. I snagged a coupon from the mailroom bulletin board for ten dollars off any meal." I just hoped I had the darn thing in my handbag.

"Gosh, it must be an expensive place," said Rashawna. "I hardly ever pay ten dollars for a whole meal, let alone that much off."

"Well, we deserve something a step up, I think," I said to happy nods all around.

We found my car, and Joel did a quick check of the interior before we got in. He and Rashawna hopped into the back seat and snuggled down together. I wasn't quite sure I liked the chauffeur role, but I let it go. We pulled onto the highway and headed north. The temperature had been going up all day, and I hoped our October snow would melt away and leave a more normal autumn for us. I had a brief mental flash from my childhood of the year we trick-or-treated in a late October snow. That had been a freaky kind of year, too. My mother had me so bundled up, it was hard to tell if I was a ghost or a snowball.

It didn't take us long to get to the restaurant, and we got out of the car, eager to see what it had to offer. There were a good number of cars in the lot, and the kitchen fans were blowing the delectable cooking scents of barbeque, garlic and warm bread into the night air. A neon sign outlining the name of the place, Rib Shack, blazed over the entrance.

"Mmm, smells good," said Rashawna.

"I hope it tastes as good as it smells," said Joel. He opened the monster wooden entry door, and we were heartily greeted by—Briscoe. He popped up from a table near the door, where he was sitting with an older woman. He introduced his mother to us. She had a full mouth, but she smiled and nodded before turning back to her plate of glistening ribs.

"Minnie! Wow, good to see you," said Briscoe. "Mom and I have come here almost every Sunday night since this place opened." He looked around and then leaned toward us. "Not such a wild crowd on Sundays, you know," he said in a hushed voice. Mom grinned at us as she wiped a bit of barbeque sauce off her lip. Then she tucked into her coleslaw with gusto.

I introduced Briscoe to Rashawna and Joel. They smiled and said hello, and just before we had to think up more small talk, the restaurant hostess rescued us. Our good luck.

"Order the double rack," said Briscoe, kissing his fingers to the air for emphasis. "You get extra slaw with that, too." He sat back down with Mom, and we quickly followed the hostess to the other side of the room. I glanced back at them, and Briscoe pointed with glee to his plate, kissing his fingers again. Sheesh.

"Seems like a nice guy," said Rashawna, "good to his mama. I like that."

The restaurant interior was pure log cabin décor, complete with log-y looking walls where old rifles (fake, I hoped) hung next to dangling powder horns. There were butter churns in the corners and barrel chairs around rough-hewn tables covered with red checkered tablecloths. We walked beneath a suspended birch bark canoe on the way to our table. Was that Joel humming the theme from the old Disney Davy Crockett series?

I decided to take Briscoe's advice and ordered the double rack of ribs, and Joel did the same. Rashawna exercised more caution and ordered a pulled pork sandwich with fries.

"Uh, I know we're not talking about the case," said Joel, "but I do want to know how it went for you this morning, Rashawna." He looked at her, and his eyes held hers.

"It wasn't too bad," she said, pouting prettily. She spread her checked napkin on her lap and, unbelievably, batted her eyelashes.

Yup, here it comes, I thought. Joel said her name, and she was all a-flutter. It was interesting to watch, and I hoped she'd say more to him than she had to me. That didn't happen, but Joel and I had had the same thought about the situation.

"Did you tell them about the knife?" he asked.

Rashawna pulled back. "Why does everybody want to know about that?" she said, a little steamed and with no eye batting.

"Because that could help identify this guy," said Joel.

"If they find him they could probably tell what sort of weapon made the marks where you wounded him," I offered. "It would be corroboration for your story."

"I guess I should add to my report then, huh?" Rashawna seemed resigned to the idea of admitting to that part of the story.

"We can talk about that on the way home, maybe," I said.

Joel reached over and covered Rashawna's hand with his own. "You're good for now, though, okay?"

"Okay, let's just enjoy this dinner that we deserve so much," Rashawna replied.

The waitress brought over a huge basket of warm breadsticks, an earthen crock of garlic herb butter and our drinks, frosty mugs of root beer. We dug in as though we were starving, and anything else about the police report took a back seat to our appetites. Next came our salads and a choice of five dressings. We'd just managed to get that down when our noses were overwhelmed by the fragrant scent of barbequed ribs, garlic roasted red potatoes and buttered broccolini. Boy, I'd need my little breath strips for sure after this meal, but we all enjoyed the food and considered it a fitting end to our weekend of toil and terror.

"Man, this place rocks," said Joel. He'd picked his ribs clean and was mopping up sauce with what was left of the garlic bread. "Good choice, Min."

I pushed away from the table and tried to smother a not very ladylike belch. "I think I'm going to need a take home box; these portions are enormous." When the waitress returned with foam boxes for our leftovers, my gaze wandered to a couple passing behind her. Something about the man caught my eye. Where had I seen him?

"Hey, I think that's Eddie from the fish fry," said Joel. He and Rashawna sat across from me at the table and had a better view of the couple. Joel tilted his nose up ever so slightly. "Smells a little like the deep fat fryer."

"That's it," I said, "a familiar face out of place." The waitress left to get the dessert menu, and I watched Eddie and the woman as they entered the bar area of the restaurant.

"I've always wondered where people who work in cafes and diners go to eat," said Rashawna. "His date could sure use a sample of that Brilliance shampoo."

"I wonder if he's married," I said. "One thing for sure, he's not at home getting all worked up about the fugitive in his upstairs apartment."

"Eddie might have kicked them out already," said Joel. "He didn't seem too happy that they were there. Selena was cussing at him big time when they busted into his back room. She said the guy with her was drunk, and they only wanted to crash there for the night."

"He must still be bleeding from when I got him with the knife," said Rashawna. She covered her mouth and looked around. "What if he dies up there?"

"I didn't actually see the guy's face at the store or at the café. He may not even be the guy who grabbed you," said Joel.

"Yeah, but there was blood in that store, and then you saw them not too long after that and then ..." Saucer-eyed Rashawna was enjoying a horror fest of the imagination.

"He's probably fine, just a little weak, maybe," I said. "But for sure they're hiding something."

"You know, there's something about Eddie that's been bugging me, like in the back of my mind," said Joel, his face a mask of concentration.

"Your little stakeout has added another dimension to this whole weird case," I said.

"The case from outer space," Rashawna said and rolled her eyes at her own bad rhyme. Then she giggled.

"Our special dessert tonight is a brownie caramel nut sundae," said the waitress, who apparently popped up through the floorboards to jolt us out of our intense discussion.

"Oh, that sounds wonderful," I said, hand up, as though holding off another onslaught of delectable dishes, "but I just can't manage it."

The waitress turned to Joel and Rashawna. "I'm out," said Rashawna.

"I'm in," said Joel, "and could I have a big glass of milk with that?"

"Whipped cream, too?"

"Oh, sure, pile it on."

"Where are you going to put it?" I asked incredulously.

"I have an idea."

"Yeah, but do you have an extra stomach?" asked Rashawna.

"Be right back with that," said the waitress.

Joel leaned in to Rashawna. "While I'm power eating that brownie thing, I want you to use the ladies' room."

"You do?"

"Yeah, it's right through the bar back there," said Joel, nodding in that direction. "Don't look!" he barked as Rashawna craned her neck. "First rule of a covert operation, babe, is not to look at your mark under any circumstances."

Boy, was he laying it on thick. I stifled another belch and settled back to listen. I was pretty sure what his idea was.

"This is sounding kinda hairy scary," said Rashawna.

"It won't be in any way scary," said Joel. "Just pay attention. Now, maybe you can get a good look at our fry cook and his lady."

"Why do you want me to do it?" asked Rashawna, arching an eyebrow in my direction.

"Because he won't remember you," said Joel. "He'd recognize me or Minnie. We've been at his place more than once."

Rashawna sighed. "Okay, okay, what am I supposed to be looking for?"

"Not looking so much as listening. Order a drink at the bar and see if you can overhear anything."

"Oh, no," said Rashawna. "I don't think I can do that. Every bartender I ever saw thinks I'm just a kid. He won't serve me, I'll bet."

"I was just thinking of something along these lines, Joel," I said. "Now, Rashawna, I think you can do this. Just act like you're twenty-one. Put on your dignity," I said. "Don't do anything ditzy, just linger a bit and see what happens. You can do sophisticated, I know you can." I handed her a five-dollar bill for the drink. "Get an Irish coffee, and bring it back to the table. I'll drink it."

"What about going to the ladies' room?"

"Make out like you don't know where it is," Joel continued. "That way you can look all over the bar. Okay, this is the covert part where you do look until you spot where Eddie and the chick are."

"Then when you come out of the ladies' room, go to the place at the bar that's closest to them," I said, warming to the intrigue of it. "Order the Irish coffee and hang out there for a few minutes and just listen. Think of yourself as a World War II undercover spy."

"Well …"

Joel winked at her. "You can do it, Curly. That Miss Marple that Minnie is always trying to be would be so on your side." Then he winked at me, the devil.

Rashawna smiled and touched her curls. I was beginning to understand that this curl touching was a sign of her resolve to get on with the situation at hand. That and pants smoothing.

The waitress returned with Joel's brownie caramel nut sundae and placed it in front of him along with a huge, frothy glass of milk. The sundae covered most of a large white plate. Joel groaned and looked at Rashawna. "Well?" he said. "Are you going or not?"

"I'll go. I guess I could get into the spy thing," said Rashawna, standing and smoothing, "but if Eddie looks at me even a little bit funny, I'm outta there."

"That's my girl," said Joel. He picked up his spoon and began climbing Brownie Mountain.

I fervently hoped there wasn't any bran in the brownie.

Joel had about half the dessert gone before Rashawna was back. She set the Irish coffee in front of me. "She was in there, in the bathroom. She's his sister. Today is her birthday, and Eddie's treating her to dinner." Rashawna bounced into her seat and tried to keep her excitement a notch below nuclear.

"Wow," said Joel, obviously impressed. "So she opened right up and talked to you, huh?" He gave up the battle with the brownie and laid the spoon to rest.

"I did some super war spy stuff. Oh, who was that chick, Mata Mary or something? Anyway, when she came out of the stall to wash her hands, I told her I loved her hair. My stomach was kicking up a little, but then we got to talking about shampoo, and I told her about Brilliance and how it was going to be on the market soon, and if she wanted a great coupon or a sample ..."

"Uh, babe?" said Joel, interrupting her. "That was a stroke of genius, but did she mention Eddie at all?"

"Oh, well, I was really cagey like. I told her I noticed the guy she came in with, and she said, 'Oh, yeah, he's my brother, and it's my birthday, so we're trying this place'. Then I said, real smooth, 'He looks familiar to me', and you know what she said?" Rashawna was near to bursting with the revelation. "She said, 'Eddie Rodriquez owns Mack's Pier, ever been there?'"

"Rodriquez?" Joel and I said together, gaping at her.

"I know," said Rashawna, her voice lowered. "Can you believe it? I almost lost it right there, but I grabbed back my sophisticated just in time. I told her I hadn't ever heard of the place but would try it because she mentioned it. Then I walked real ladylike out of there."

No wonder she was excited. Not only had she successfully ordered a drink at the bar, but because of her ladies' room visit, it seemed we'd stumbled into a whole nest of Rodriquez renegades. I was pretty sure we'd find that truck still sitting in the fish fry driveway if we dared drive past it after this.

"So how'd I do?" asked Rashawna.

"You were excellent," I said. "We are so hot on this case. Now, as long as Eddie's here for dinner, I think we should go back and see if that truck is still in the driveway at the fish fry."

"Anything else?" said the pop-up waitress. She had our check already made up and waved it through the air like she wasn't sure who to give it to.

"Oh, no, just the check," I said, snatching it from her. She strolled to her next station.

"I think it's a great idea to check for the truck," said Joel. "If it's still there, we can call the police. There's plenty to tell now."

I dug around in my handbag and took out my wallet. My credit card would take a beating on this one. Even though I had a coupon and the food wasn't that expensive, I was paying for three full dinners with drinks and a dessert. Plus the Irish coffee was five bucks! I sighed. Well, what else did I have to spend my money on? The waitress came back and took my card. I'd included a tip for her on the bill. She returned with my receipt, smiling, and I signed for our meal. Then I grabbed my take-out box and stood.

"How long are we going to be, I mean, checking out that truck?" Rashawna looked back into the bar just in time to see Eddie and his sister being escorted to a table.

Good. They'd be at least an hour. "Not that long," I said. When we walked outside I noticed the air had become distinctly warmer. Our snow wouldn't last long if this kept up. October was one of those months, like April, that could turn on a dime when it came to the weather.

"So, now, what are we gonna do if we see the truck?" asked Rashawna.

"I think we'll have a good reason to call Dan," I said. "If nothing else they'll be able to arrest Joe for abducting you." I took my keys out of my handbag and glanced around the parking lot for my Toyota. At the moment I spotted the car, I also saw someone standing near it. My heart got a little jolt of adrenaline, and Joel spotted the person at the same time. He opened his mouth to yell, but the person moved away, and it was soon evident that he was simply looking for his own vehicle. I let out a garlic-laden sigh of relief.

Rashawna, on the other hand, had taken no notice and trotted full on to the passenger side door. She threw it open and slid across the seat. Joel hesitated briefly as he scoped out the cars around us, and then all hell broke loose in the form of Rashawna's screaming. Her ear-piercing wail was soon followed by a Dollar Store bag hurtling out the car door at Joel.

He picked it up from the ground, looked in, gasped and handed it to me. Inside was a whole bunch of Taffy Tails, all bound up with a red shoelace.

Twenty

Joel jumped in beside Rashawna. I flung the Dollar Store bag into the car, got in and slammed the door. At this point Rashawna was hyperventilating. Joel was doing his best to settle her down. Now what? I didn't get a good look at the guy who'd been standing by my car, but he could have been just another customer. Had Eddie put the bag in my car before he came into the restaurant with his sister, and why would he? Another adrenaline rush hit as I turned the car over and gunned the engine. Then I stopped. I took my foot off the gas pedal and shut the car off. A new emotion was rearing its head—rage.

"Minnie, what are you doing?" Rashawna was shaking so hard the car was jiggling.

"I know what she's doing," said Joel, feeling it too. "You're mad, aren't you, Min?"

"I sure am."

"I'm with you there," said Joel. "I'm getting real tired of being terrorized for some reason I have no clue about."

I nodded my head and turned to face them. Our voices seemed to be having a calming effect on Rashawna. Joel had his arm around her, and she'd stopped shaking. "Rashawna, do you have your house key with you?" I asked.

"I think so, Minnie, hang on." She shuffled through the contents of her black hobo handbag and jangled them up from the depths. "Yup, right here. Why?"

"We're going to your place and figure this thing out."

"I don't know if that's such a good idea, Minnie," she whispered. "What if somebody's watching the place?"

"I think I have a better idea," said Joel. "We can go to my place."

Okay, this caught me by surprise. So far, Joel hadn't even mentioned that he had a place, never mind asking us to go there. I'd imagined him bumming beds from friends and doing an occasional all-nighter on a bus bench.

"Where do you live?" asked Rashawna as she pulled away, startled.

Joel coughed. "Loudonville."

"Loudonville!" Rashawna and I said together.

"Okay, here's the thing," said Joel. "It's really my dad's place. I have an apartment off the main house, and he's just let me back into it."

"Joel, honey, its mostly only rich people who live in Loudonville," said Rashawna. Her voice had gone from full of fear to full of awe in about two seconds.

"Why has your father just let you back in?" I asked.

"Because I got my car back," replied Joel. "Dad is a real hardass about making your own way in this world and wants me to prove I can. He's been down on me ever since I dropped out of college a couple of years back."

"All right," I said, "we can get into more of this later. Let's go. We'll probably be safer at your place anyhow. Right now, I want you to tell me which way to turn when we leave this parking lot." I restarted the car and began backing up.

"Left," said Joel. "We're only about ten or twelve minutes away."

It wasn't long before we were driving through a lovely residential neighborhood, and Joel began rattling off street names. Four turns later we pulled into a tree-lined horseshoe drive in front of a two-story, brick almost-mansion that loomed out of the darkness.

"There's a shorter driveway just off to the side of the house there," said Joel, pointing past a row of trimmed hedges bordered by solar garden lights.

Behind the house, at the end of a covered, glass-enclosed patio, was an attached room that looked about the size of a two-car garage. I stopped the car, and Joel opened the car door on his side. Rashawna didn't move.

"Come on," Joel said to me and began walking toward the front door. There was a small, black Colonial lamppost lighting the brick walkway. Joel fished a key out of his back pocket and put it into the lock.

I poked my head into the back seat and gave Rashawna the *come on* sign with my hand.

"I can't, Minnie," she whispered.

"What's wrong?"

"I didn't know he was rich," she said.

"Um, you never noticed how he's always short on funds? Besides, what difference would that make even if he was?" Joel had gone inside, and lights came on as he went from room to room inside the garage apartment.

"I never dated a rich guy before. I don't know how to."

"Rashawna," I hissed, "get out of the car. You can figure out rich guy dating after we get this shoelace thing solved."

That brought our purpose to her mind, and she put one leg out the door and then the other. She slapped at her pants. Good. Now we were getting somewhere.

"You two coming?" Joel called from the doorway.

"Yup, we are," I said, prodding Rashawna along the walkway.

I smelled coffee as we stepped into Joel's living room, which bordered on the bizarre. There was a beautiful, cordovan-colored leather couch on the one unbroken wall, and next to that was a vintage 1970s pole lamp, bumpy gold globes and all. The Navajo white walls were bare, but the taupe-colored sculpted carpeting was exquisite and looked almost new. There was nothing else in the room. Joel returned to us and said he had coffee brewing. "I have one of those cool coffee makers that always has hot water in it. Push a button and bam, coffee in minutes."

He chattered like a food channel salesman. "Sounds good, Joel," I said as he went back into the tiny kitchen. "Whenever someone's making coffee or tea, things don't seem so bad somehow."

"Oh, I like that, Minnie," said Rashawna. She looked around the room. "Not much in here, is there?" She ran her hand over the leather couch. "This is nice, though."

Joel came through from the kitchen, carrying a bamboo tray. Three cups of coffee, a sugar shaker and a quart of milk sat next to a pile of napkins and some spoons on the tray.

"Sorry, I know you really love tea," he said. He set the tray on the arm of the leather sofa and held up one finger. "Be right back." He scooted back to the kitchen and reappeared with a wooden snack tray. He put the coffee tray on top and motioned for us to sit. He sat cross-legged on the floor in front of us.

"That's just fine, Joel. We're switch drinkers," I said. "This is very interesting." I glanced around the room.

"Huh, is that what you call it?" said Rashawna, obviously no longer thinking Joel was undatably rich. With only a few concessions to the finer things in life, the room had the feeling of waiting for prosperity rather than blatantly showing it.

"My dad again," said Joel. "I've gotta earn every dime to furnish this place."

"Great couch," said Rashawna, plopping down. "Smart dad."

I sat beside her and took a cup of coffee. "What does your father do, Joel, if it's okay to ask?"

"No problem asking. He's a doctor, an orthopedist. Works a lot with kids."

"Very cool," said Rashawna.

"He kind of came up the hard way. Put himself through college and medical school, so he's not real happy about what I'm doing right now."

"Yeah, I guess there's not much future in the dollar store business," said Rashawna.

"I'm only there until after Christmas, then I have plans."

"That's good to know. Maybe you can fill us in on that sometime, but for now let's get on with it," I said. "Joel, I have a question for you."

"Shoot."

"You've had time to think about this whole affair. Do you have any clue why Roberto sat outside the Dollar Store staring at you for two days?"

"Here's what I'm thinking, Min," said Joel. He took a slurp of the coffee and did that baseball neck crank thing again.

Uh, oh. That nervous little movement caught my eye and made me ask a question. "Wait," I said, holding my hand up. "Joel, is there any reason Roberto would have suspected you of being the killer?"

"Okay, here's what I'm thinking, Min," he repeated.

"There's a reason why we're involved in all this."

"Yup, and here's maybe why," he coughed again. "I may have let it slip that I once dated Jennifer Landis."

Rashawna and I turned to each other, turned to Joel and turned back, speechless. This was big, scary news. *Be Miss Marple, be Miss Marple.* I took a deep breath, "And how did that go?" Deep breath, smile sweetly, be calm.

"Okay, don't either of you panic. I did not kill anybody." Joel was emphatic.

Rashawna exhibited deadly calm and said, "That's not what Minnie asked about. How did your relationship with Jennifer Landis go?"

"It went for about four dates. I mean, she was beautiful, but that was it. Waaay too stuck on herself for me."

"Who did you let that information slip to?" I asked quickly. I felt Rashawna relax a little beside me.

"This has just surfaced in the old brain here," he answered, finger tapping his forehead. "A few days after I started at the Dollar Store, some of us were sitting in the back room around that little white plastic table, and I may have mentioned that I'd dated her. I don't even know what we were talking about that her name came up."

"Who was at the table?'

"Cheryl, our boss, a couple of the other clerks."

"Selena?" asked Rashawna.

"She came in for about two seconds," Joel answered. "She was on the registers then, and we were on break. Don't know if she heard anything."

"But she may have," I said. "Was that before or after you went to lunch with her?"

"Before, and lunch was her idea," he answered, "but, um, there's another thing, too."

Now what? "We're listening."

"We sure are," said Rashawna.

"I was sort of called in for questioning after Jennifer was killed." Joel looked at me, then Rashawna. "Just routine, no big deal, they had nothing on me."

"Joel," I hissed, "you're babbling."

"That's how come you know about questioning at the police station," said Rashawna. "Oh, honey, why didn't you tell me?" Her eyes were big pools of melted chocolate. Silly me, I thought she'd go ballistic on him.

I plowed on. "If Selena found that out, it may have been all she needed to throw suspicion on you," I said. "Did she try to get any information out of you at that lunch?"

"I don't remember a lot about that lunch," said Joel. "I'll bet she's been following this story for a long time, though."

"And I'll bet you anything she knows or suspects who the real killer is," I said. "She may even be protecting someone."

"Suppose Roberto, our stalker, was watching you and Selena because Selena was leading him that way."

"To throw suspicion off the real killer, the one she's protecting?" Joel's eyebrows shot up. "Well, thank you, Miss Evil."

"There's been a bit of renewed interest in the red shoelace killer in the last few weeks. Maybe Roberto knew something about that, too, saw the piece in the paper to back up Selena's lies about you. I'm almost positive he was the one who went into the new shoe store, asking about the gray sneakers with the red shoelaces. Gretchen, the salesgirl, said he had a scrunchy forehead."

"That's right," said Rashawna. "Remember, I said something was wrong with his forehead when he looked at me the other day? His hair was all shoved down almost to his eyes, but there was definitely something going on with that forehead!"

"Remember, too, the EMT's remark about the cysts on Roberto's forehead," I said.

Rashawna snapped her fingers, "Right again, Minnie. Poor guy," she said. "I'll bet that did a number on his ego."

"Okay, so Roberto is—was—the mall stalker and was checking out all the places where there might be red shoelaces."

"You think he thought Joel was buying them?" asked Rashawna.

"Could be. There were red shoelaces at the Dollar Store counter, you'll remember, and it's probably why he followed Joel out to the parking lot," I said.

"The way I see it, we've got two suspects, and I ain't one of them," said Joel. "Those three guys, Eddie, Joe and Roberto, the dead guy, all have the same last name. That says something."

Rashawna and I looked blankly at him. "But why would Roberto even care about who the killer is?" I asked. "That's what's really puzzling me."

"Was *he* the killer?" asked Joel. "Somebody found out and got him in the parking lot?"

I had a thought. "What if there was a love connection? What if Roberto, the dead guy, was watching over Selena? What if he had a thing for her?" I remembered their confrontation in the Hannaford parking lot. He'd warned her but didn't harm her.

"There's not too many guys like that around," said Joel emphatically. "My money is on Joe or Eddie for the killer. I don't know about the love thing."

"Joel, you called Selena evil that night outside of the police station. Why?" I asked.

"Min, what would you say about a person who never, ever smiles? Someone who acts like she hates the world, especially customers, and someone who has a rattlesnake tattoo on her upper thigh?"

"Upper thigh?" said Rashawna. She leveled her gaze on Joel with an expression that, if bottled, would have been a best seller to every suspicious wife and girlfriend in the country.

"She wore shorts, really short shorts, to work one day at the end of summer," Joel said hastily. "It was on her inner, upper thigh, too." Joel shivered.

"Inner, upper thigh?" Rashawna spit the words out and drew herself up on the sofa.

"I hate tattoos, really," said Joel, "but that thing was causing all kinds of trouble, especially with the guy customers. I mean, she's built like a tank, and with that tat showing, well, her register just got way too crowded. Guys would come in and buy a pack of gum just to get a look. The boss decided to send her home to change. Just before she left I saw her in the employees' lounge, laying some really nasty language on him while she crashed through her handbag, looking for her keys."

"Huh," said Rashawna, appeased a little. "Guess her favorite F-word isn't *free* or *fantastic* then."

"You know, an odd little thought just occurred to me," I said. "Is it possible Selena's the one in danger right now?"

"You mean, is she holed up in an upstairs apartment over a fish fry place with a husband who abducts people out of their own house and also is maybe a murderer?" asked Rashawna.

"That's exactly what I'm thinking," I said. "When Roberto, the dead guy, confronted her in the parking lot the other night, maybe he was warning her. He said something about her being next."

"And maybe he was warning her because of Joel?" asked Rashawna. "Like she was going to be Joel's next victim?"

"Selena does bear a resemblance to the murder victim. If Roberto cared about Selena, he would have been on the lookout for anybody around her: Joel, her husband Joe, maybe even Eddie."

"I tried to be nice to the woman but not in any romantic way," said Joel, shaking his head. "I think she has that rattlesnake tat because she's one herself."

"Besides," said Rashawna, "what would that have to do with this shoelace killer?"

"That's where it gets interesting," I said. "We know that the murdered woman was young, had long dark hair and went to the high school near where her body was found. Suppose the Rodriquez guys were all from around here and maybe went to the same high school."

Joel stood up and jabbed the air with his fist. "That's it!"

Rashawna and I looked at him. "The guy who owns the Mack's Pier, Eddie? I went to high school with him. Man, it's been driving me crazy. He's changed a lot in the last few years, so it's taken me this long to figure out where I'd seen him. It's been working around in here all week." He made finger circles near his left temple.

"What about the other two?" I asked. "Joe and Roberto have the same last name as Eddie. What's the relationship, cousins, maybe?"

"I never got a close look at Joe or Roberto. That's why I wasn't making any connections," said Joel. "The clowns, that's what everyone called them," said Joel. His eyes were dancing around, remembering high school, then glazing over as he drifted into a not-too-distant past.

"Because of their feet, I'll bet," said Rashawna.

"I was two years behind them. Eddie was a senior, and his brother Joe and cousin Roberto were both juniors. I remember they all sort of hung out together. There were those girls, one was Jennifer, who were pretty brutal when it came to making fun of them. The clowns, yeah, the big feet." Joel smiled at Rashawna. "You've got it, Rashawna."

"Was Selena in high school with all of you?" I asked.

"I'm not sure. If she was a freshman, maybe, I wouldn't have noticed her."

I stood up. "She must know the three of them somehow. When I spoke with Cheryl, she told me Selena had it pretty rough growing up. My guess is she was in high school with all of you but in the lower grades. And tough as Selena is, I think she may be in grave danger. If that truck is still parked behind Mack's, I'll have to call Dan and tell him what I know."

"What's this I stuff?" asked Joel. "You going somewhere?"

"If you are, I'm going, too," said Rashawna. "Besides, you have to take us back to the mall to get Joel's car."

"You're right, I forgot about that. Okay, kids, I guess we started this together," I said, "so let's finish it together, too."

Joel took our cups back into the kitchen, doused the lights in his apartment, and we all trooped back out to the car. He let Rashawna get in ahead of him, and then he looked at me.

"Why do you think Selena's in trouble?"

"Because she's too evil not to be," I said.

Twenty-One

I concentrated on my breathing as I drove, in through the nose, out through the mouth. I'd had enough adrenaline rushes for one night. Joel and Rashawna hardly spoke as we turned out of the peaceful neighborhood where Joel lived on our way to face down a maniacal killer. Okay, I had to stop thinking like that. Of course, I did subscribe to the old maxim, "Never corner a dog that's meaner than you are," but all we intended to do was confirm that the blue Ford was still at Mack's. After that the cops could take over. No junkyard dogs in our plan, no sir.

Mack's Pier was on Fisher Drive, but I decided to park a block away. We got out of the car, and I locked it. "Joel, do you have your flashlight with you?" I asked.

"Yup, right here on my key fob," he answered.

We could see the fish fry on Fisher as we walked toward the restaurant and rounded the street corner. I noticed a light in the upstairs apartment above the Mack's Pier sign. Fisher Street was fairly well lit, but the surrounding side streets tended to the dark side. What a difference from the neighborhood we'd just left. We trotted three abreast up the street, and as we neared the front of the restaurant, a set of truck headlights popped on from the side street opposite us. We did a quick deer-in-the-headlights and then launched a class A impression of terrified cockroaches as we bolted for the dark shadows beneath a nearby giant oak.

"Move, move, move!" I barked.

"Oh no, oh no, oh no," gabbled Rashawna. She hustled along beside me in her clunky, not-good-for-running shoes and ducked behind the massive tree trunk, Joel at her heels. At that moment the truck swung out onto the road. We had a quick glimpse of a saggy-faced, middle-aged blonde woman with a cigarette dangling from her bottom lip as she roared off down the road. We all exhaled at once.

"That was close," I whispered. "Okay, let's calm down for a few seconds, and then we'll execute our plan."

"If we had a plan, I think it just got executed, pow!" said Joel as he and Rashawna huddled in the shadows with me. I held my palm to my chest and tried to think of what to do next.

"We had ten whole minutes to discuss a plan on the way over here, and we all sat in the car like log lumps," said Rashawna.

"You mean bumps on a log," said Joel.

"It's such a dumb saying, like, when did you last see log lumps?"

"Bumps, the saying goes, like a bump on a log." Joel sighed, exasperated.

"Excuse me, you two, but we have a killer's truck to identify."

We all poked our heads around the tree trunk, Joel's neck craning the farthest.

"Did either of you see the truck in the driveway?" I asked.

"I only saw the truck with the headlights and the old lady with the coffin nail hangin' off her lip," said Rashawna.

"Then we'll just have to go and take a look," I said, ignoring her. "Come on." I stepped out from behind our great oaken shield and hustled over the sidewalk toward the side of the building. The two of them followed me like ducklings as we hugged the faux brick storefront. While creeping past the big front windows, we had a glimpse of a low light burning somewhere in the back of the kitchen area. The dim bulb inside gave the restaurant interior an eerie glow, and the theme from *Tales from the Crypt* drifted briefly through my hyper-alert brain. Then we were in the driveway, which turned out to be gravel and made a horrible crunching sound as we walked. "Softer, walk softer," I directed.

"This would be where the killer throws on the porch light, jumps out and starts firing," whimpered Rashawna.

"I can't believe how much noise this stuff makes," whispered Joel, "like a little kid power crunching his Space-O's cereal."

We all tried to lighten our tread as we came up on the hulking object in front of us.

There was a vehicle parked there all right. "Joel," I whispered, "turn on your flashlight."

"Right, Min," Joel whispered back. His key fob clinked, and he muttered as he fought with the flashlight switch. When it came on, it didn't give much light, but it would have to do.

Rashawna grabbed for the back of my coat, clutching a wad of the fabric. "Don't worry, Minnie, I'm okay," she said, but I could feel her whole body trembling. She didn't let go. Joel stepped in front of me as we approached the back of the truck. He lifted the tarp and directed his flashlight at the license plate.

"Orange tea bag 843!" cried Rashawna.

"Shhhhh," Joel and I said together.

Joel lifted the tarp a little farther. "Yup, same as when I was here before. And something else, too."

Rashawna and I peered over the edge of the truck bed and gasped. Two human-shaped bundles lay motionless, feet sticking out from the old blankets in which they were wrapped, with no movement coming from either one of them.

"That's it!" I screeched. "Back to the car! Back to the car! We're calling the police!" I looked furtively around and began digging in my handbag as I crunched out of the driveway and fled down the sidewalk. Rashawna's chunky shoes did a brisk rat-a-tat on the pavement behind me, and Joel's quickened breath trailed in the crisp air like locomotive steam as he raced to keep up with us. We all hit the car at once. Each of us jerked upright as we grabbed a door handle on the car that, this time, I'd decided to lock.

Rashawna yanked on the handle. "Let me in!"

"There you are," I said as my keys found my hand. I only shook a little as I tried to unlock the doors. The two seconds it took to open them seemed like two hours, but the instant the lock clicked we piled in and slammed the doors shut.

By force of habit I paused to put my seatbelt on, no easy task on my hundred and seventy pound frame, but that was a big mistake. There was a sudden, sharp rap on the passenger side window. I turned and found myself looking down the barrel of a gun.

That was my second encounter with a gun that week, and I was a little tired of it, but I had a feeling this one wasn't plastic like the one Joel had poked at me a few days ago.

"Eek!" Rashawna managed to make this one little sound before she passed out cold on Joel's shoulder. The door was yanked open, and suddenly we had an unwanted passenger.

"We should have locked ourselves in," Joel hissed from the back seat.

"Drive the car," the intruder said. He wore a black knit cap low over his head and sounded as though he was trying to disguise his voice.

My hands shook so badly I wasn't sure I could drive. I touched the steering wheel, and there was audible dull thudding as I tried to control my trembling.

"Come on, come on," said the gunman, waving the revolver in my face.

Oh, great, an impatient madman with murder on his mind. Calmed me right down. Then I had a blinding flash. I held my keys up. "Uh, these are the wrong keys," I said insanely, thinking a little faster now. Um, he'd just seen me open the car door with them. "I keep the actual car key on another ring, hang on." I plunged my hand into my handbag and thrashed around inside. Then I felt it--my cell phone. Oh, bless you, Radio Shack Jimmy, for talking me into getting a cell phone. Maybe I could turn it on and press four without calling attention to it.

"Ouch!" I yelled as I quickly pressed one button and then the other. "Heh, heh, safety pin," I said as I pulled out my finger and sucked on it for a few seconds. Number four on my cell was Detective Horowitz's direct line, and I hoped he'd pick up and hang on. "Minnie" would show on his display, and I'd try to make enough noise to get his attention.

"Okay, okay, I found my keys," I gasped, jangling them for him to see. "Where are we going?" I dropped my handbag gently beside the gas pedal and sent up a quick prayer.

"Lady, just drive, I'll tell you when to stop." He slapped his palm on the dashboard.

"Okay, but which way shall I turn?" I said a little too loudly.

"I'm not deaf," Black Cap yelled back. "Turn left out of this street. I said I'll tell you when to stop."

"Okay, I'll turn left," I said with great emphasis. "Shall I go back past Mack's Pier, the fish fry place?" This got me a suspicious glare from the killer, and I smiled as sweetly as I could even though my rib dinner was threatening to come up. I took several deep breaths—nose inhale, mouth exhale—and concentrated on backing up. I turned left as we pulled out of the street and headed back up the road toward Mack's. I glanced into the restaurant driveway as we passed, and to my horror I saw the tarp rise from the truck bed. Someone was climbing out of it.

Twenty-Two

I could have sworn the two bodies in the back of that pickup were dead, but I didn't have much time for idle pondering, because my immediate task was to figure out how to come out of this alive. I did the breathing thing again and wondered what Agatha would have me do were I one of her characters. I tried not to hyperventilate as I thought of old millstreams and quaint, blood-covered ... uh, vine-covered cottages.

A groan came from the back seat. Rashawna was coming back to life. I glanced in the rear view mirror and saw Joel put his arm protectively around her. He was also staring hard at the man beside me. Good boy, I thought, try to figure out the identity of this creep. Mack's Pier wasn't exactly in the best part of town, and I followed the signs for I-90. Jimmy had assured me that my cell phone would function at peak performance on the Interstate highways, where so many of the cell towers were located. I wanted that more than anything right now.

"Not that way, lady," said our abductor. He glanced up the street and waved his stupid gun some more. "Stay on this street."

Uh oh, this was the part where he directs me to a back alley, pops all three of us, and we aren't found until some nosy collie notices the stink and runs the news home to Timmy.

"You mean on Rapp Road just up ahead?" I raised my voice again and strained to see a street sign. I was pretty sure we were near Rapp Road.

"I said I'm not deaf. Just drive!"

His anger was feeding his annoyed shouting, and I hoped Dan would hear that, too. "So what's your name?" Oh, right. Good one, Minnie, because this guy seemed just like the kind of killer who would share that information. Maybe I could ask him his favorite color, too.

"Drive." His voice was lower and more threatening this time. He raised the gun.

I decided to memorize everything about him and keep my mouth shut. He was about my height, maybe an inch or two taller. As we passed each streetlight I was able to pick up on several other physical attributes. A few strands of dark hair had escaped the knit cap, and his lantern-jawed face was smooth. He was probably still in his twenties. Something was dinging in the back of my head. He wore jeans and a black t-shirt and a dark leather jacket with the collar pulled up around his ears. I glanced at his feet. They were huge! Then I had it. This was Eddie, fish fry Eddie. Where the devil had he come from? We'd left him at the rib place. Had he abandoned his sister to pursue us? My mind was rife with possible scenarios. There was a sudden disturbance in the back seat.

"Awww!" Rashawna was fully awake now and gasping. Two seconds later I understood the reason for her distress. The interior of my car was filled with an overpowering stench. I became a little light in the head as I attempted to employ another breathing strategy, holding my breath.

"Geez, man, control yourself!" Eddie held his free hand over his face as he shot a look into the back seat.

My eyes began to water. I dared a gasp or two.

"Must have been the nuts in that brownie sundae," said Joel. "Some things give me awful gas."

"Roll down a window," gasped Rashawna.

"Stop the car," the gunman ordered, "now! Stop!"

I pulled into a small parking lot that bordered on a kiddy park. Unbelievably, it had been plowed, and I could see that children had been playing here recently, probably because school had been closed right after our October storm. This gave me some hope that the neighborhood was one where folks were out and about and active, that it was not some drug dealer-infested, rat hole of a place. Still, I wasn't too happy to get out into the cold.

Eddie was the first one out of the car. He darted around and pulled my door open. "Out!" He used the gun as an indicator. He opened the passenger side door and motioned to Joel. Rashawna had passed out again. "What's with that girl, anyway? Aw, just leave her!" he yelled.

Eddie marched Joel and me to a picnic table, and we slogged through the slush that had been churned up by the neighborhood kids and today's warmer weather. He yelled for us to sit down. I looked back at my car. All the doors were open, and Rashawna was slumped over in the back seat.

Joel didn't take his eyes off the man. A sort of recognition showed in his eyes, and then he spoke. "You're one of the clowns aren't you? You're Eddie."

Bingo! Joel had picked up on it, too. The knit cap had been pulled so low over Eddie's forehead, and his jacket collar so high, it was hard to be sure. Plus it was almost pitch dark. There was one weak light on a pole next to the kiddy park fence, but there wasn't enough illumination from it to see anything clearly. The only other things in the park were a basketball hoop on a square of pavement, some swings, and an overflowing trashcan.

"You two, shut up," said Eddie. "I'm not a clown, either." He glanced over his shoulder to where we'd pulled into the kiddy park. What was he looking for?

"Well, are we just going to sit here?" I asked.

"Did I say you could talk? We're sitting here until that stink is gone."

I had the distinct feeling that Eddie had no clue what to do next. He began to pace. I was screwing up my courage to ask him a few questions, but Joel beat me to it.

"Those girls made your life miserable in school. That's why you did it, isn't it?" Joel asked. I could tell that his mind was working all the angles, and he was getting at something.

"Shut up!" The veins in Eddie's neck stood out. He pointed the gun directly at Joel.

"I was two years behind you in school, but I remember you now. They had a name for you and your brother and cousin. Joe is your brother and Roberto is, or was, your cousin. They called you the clowns because of your feet." Joel leaned over and peered at Eddie's feet.

Bad move.

Eddie winged his gun hand across Joel's face. Joel's head snapped back, and his hand flew to his cheek. He recoiled like a snake, and when he looked up at Eddie, there was bright fury in his eyes.

"Now that'll be enough, young man!" I barked at Eddie. I was surprised at my own boldness, but I never could abide bullies. Eddie took a few steps toward me. Okay, it was time for wise and calm to kick in.

"They shouldn't have made fun of your feet," I said, holding Eddie's gaze.

He edged over to the table and sat down across from Joel and me. I could see his gun hand shaking. I hoped his bravado was failing him.

"Everybody has something wrong with them," I said. "Look at me. Do you think I want to be fifty ... uh, forty pounds overweight?" My stomach muscles contracted.

He almost laughed. The weak streetlight nearby barely allowed us to see each other. I had given up hope that Detective Horowitz would find us. My cell phone was still on the floor of the car, and I doubted he'd heard any of our conversation. I'd have to count on my wits, and they were threatening to go AWOL. The dampness from the bench was creeping into my coat and numbing my legs.

"Yeah, you're sure packin' a lotta junk in your trunk. Maybe you should cut down on the deep fried fish and vinegar fries." Eddie's eyes brightened and then showed some sign of an inner struggle. "Those girls?" he said abruptly. "They called themselves the red sweater girls. They loved to show up at school in their fancy red sweaters, like the three of 'em were in some real snooty club. On red sweater days all the other girls would suck up to them." He made a smoochy sound with his lips. "It was sickening, but they ruled the school. All of them were stuck on themselves, made fun of anybody different from them." Eddie drew a weary hand across his forehead. His back was to the car, and I looked briefly over his shoulder. I thought I saw movement near the front fender. Oh, boy, Rashawna had come around.

"That's why you used a red shoelace tied in a triple bow." I had to keep him talking. "Three girls, three bows, with one dead and two to go?" Would Rashawna have enough sense to grab the cell phone and punch 911?

"Yeah, somebody must have had it in for that one, uh, Jennifer, I think," said Eddie. "Can't say she didn't get what she deserved."

Joel must have seen Rashawna, too. Side by side on the picnic table bench I could feel the tension in both of us as we tried to keep Eddie's attention.

"Hey, Eddie, you remember Dicky Larson?" asked Joel, taking a whole different tack.

"Huh, that guy was insane," replied Eddie, squinting at Joel and lowering the gun. "It was a real special day when he didn't get in trouble. The principal was on his case all the time. Whatever happened to him?"

Eddie was taking the bait.

"Oh, man. He got hauled up to the big house. The state of New York's gonna be payin' his rent for long time." Joel attempted a macho grin.

"What'd he do ..."

Eddie never finished. A Rashawna-shaped shadow reared up behind him and landed a powerful blow to his right temple with the sack of Taffy Tails. I'd never taken them out of the car after we'd been at the rib place. Eddie went over like a hay bale in a windstorm.

"Get the phone, get the phone!" I unwedged myself from the picnic bench and raced for the car. "Joel, sit on him! Get the gun. We don't have any time to waste."

Then we heard the truck.

Twenty-Three

It looked like it was coming at us at about eighty miles an hour. Joel, Rashawna and I were stunned into inaction. Not good. Just as the driver reached the edge of the kiddy park parking lot, the truck hit an icy patch and skidded sideways. The driver hit the brakes and did a full doughnut. As the back of the truck swung crazily around, we saw a figure jouncing around inside the truck bed.

"Help, she's crazy!" the person yelled. "Help!" His arms thrashed, and his hands grabbed at the truck sides as he tried to hold onto the old blanket wrapped around his body.

Rashawna gasped. "That's him!" She flapped her hands back and forth. "That's the guy who took me!" She ran to Joel's side and clung to his arm.

It had to be Joe, Selena's husband, which meant Selena was driving the truck. She jerked it to a stop and barreled out of the driver's side door, swinging a shotgun in her hand as she ran towards us. She looked like an angry Amazon on steroids. Really, really not good.

"Stop right where you are, Selena!" yelled Joel. He gently removed Rashawna's hand from his arm and plucked Eddie's revolver from his stricken form. He laid it across the top of his arm. He reminded me of something you'd see in a bad spy movie. I would have laughed if I hadn't been so paralyzed with fear.

She kept coming.

"Selena!" Joel wasn't backing down.

Rashawna had run to my side and was now clutching my arm. We clung to each other and watched, popeyed, as Selena marched on. Under her breath Rashawna said, "Joe," and sure enough, there was Joe, somehow out of the truck and moving. He'd untangled himself from the blanket and was bent as though in pain. We tried to watch without showing it as Joe staggered up behind Selena. But she must have sensed something, because she whirled and raised the shotgun, taking aim just as Joe burst from the ground and dove, taking her out at the knees. They went down howling. The shotgun flew from Selena's grasp and jettisoned into the air. Rashawna took off. I would never have thought she could run so fast in those shoes, but she reached Selena in about fifteen seconds and managed to be in the perfect position as the shotgun plunged earthward.

"Got it, Minnie!" Rashawna yelled with glee, holding it over her head. She turned and charged back to the table. At the same time Joel rushed up from the bench, gun still pointed, and hurried past her to Selena and Joe. It was like some perfectly choreographed ballet of the bizarre. Rashawna looked at the shotgun, now safely out of the reach of the furious Selena. "Man, you could kill somebody with this thing," she said and laid it down gingerly. There was blood on the butt.

"Set them down over here, Joel," I said as he hustled Selena and Joe back to the picnic table. "I'll get my cell and call the police." I hurried over to my car and grabbed the phone from the floor on the driver's side.

"Minnie?" said a voice as I picked it up.

"Dan!" I blurted. "I can hardly believe this. You're on the line."

"Yes, yes I am, Minnie, and all because you called," he chuckled. "How's that new cell phone working out for you?"

Obviously he hadn't heard anything from inside the car during our crazy ride to the kiddy park. I could hear the mirth in his voice, but that quickly dissipated as I rushed to tell him of our predicament. I gave him the best directions I could and described the truck. "The truck lights are on and lighting the place up."

"I'll commandeer a squad car and be there in ten," said Dan. "Can you hold them that long?"

"I think we can handle it," I said, hoping it was the truth. As I squished my way back to the picnic table, I wondered just what the truth was about the three people we were guarding. Joel had used his belt to bind Selena and Joe. Eddie was still out cold. Those Taffy Tails must have been stale as all get out to knock him out like that.

"Police will be here in ten minutes," I said, sitting down opposite Selena and Joe, who were bound back to back and straddling the picnic table bench. "Why don't we chat while we wait?" Selena's truck had come around far enough that the headlights, still on, provided a halo of light where we sat. I looked at our captives. "Which one of you killed Roberto?"

"That deformed scum! He bought all my red shoelaces," said Selena viciously.

"Selena, shut up." said Joe.

"That stupid freakazoid with the Klingon forehead. Why did he have to show up? He ruined everything." She savagely shrugged her shoulders. "Get this thing off of me!"

Joe was in a severely weakened state, but he jerked his body back and forth, trying vainly to loosen the belt.

"That first girl was just the beginning," ranted Selena. "I had plans for all of them."

"No, no, Selena, don't," Joe whimpered. His body slumped against hers. "You don't need to say this."

So the evil Selena was the killer, after all.

Selena twisted awkwardly on the bench, attempting to see Eddie. Her face softened. "Eddie?" she said to his prone form. He didn't respond. "Eddie, please be okay."

I was taken aback by the tenderness in her voice. Seeing him must have triggered an urge in Selena to confess. She began a trip down memory lane.

"When I got to my new high school, I found Eddie," she said, looking at me and ignoring Joel. "He was happy, funny, and just about the only guy in that whole place worth looking at. He had a goofy grin just like my Pop."

Okay, now I was confused. Eddie? Why was she speaking like this about Eddie?

"Well, if you were crushing so bad on Eddie, how come you're married to this here guy then?" asked Rashawna. She came around the table and stood with her hands on her hips, very secure with Joel's gun backing her up.

"Because he blackmailed me into it."

"Selena," said Joe, so soft we could barely hear it.

"When that first red sweater girl came to work at the Dollar Store, I couldn't believe it. She told me her mom thought she should mix with the simple people." Selena couldn't have sounded more disgusted. "They made me train her, and she was clueless about who I was. I'd turned out to be just as smart and pretty as her."

"Yeah, pretty like a rattlesnake," growled Rashawna, glancing at Selena's thigh area.

"But Joe knew you hated her, didn't he?" I asked, shooting a sidelong glance at the ground where Eddie lay. Selena ignored me and kept on.

"On the night I finally got my hands around her scrawny neck, this idiot comes to find me. You'd think after I told him to go date a great ape he'd have a clue, but no. " Selena jerked her head backward, knocking into Joe. He groaned once, but she didn't even wince. "It was nice and dark in that alley behind the store, and I felt the life ooze out of her. Lover boy Joe had all the answers, though." She jerked her shoulders again. "It was his golden opportunity."

Joe was silent.

"Oh, yeah. He had it all figured out and suggested dumping her at the school," Selena continued, "but the red shoelace was my idea. Pure genius, too. The clowns had the last word. They called my Eddie a clown."

I glanced at Joel, who mouthed *evil* to me.

"Selena, was Roberto in love with you, too?" I asked.

"How do I know? What if he was?"

"I saw you with him at the Hannaford a few nights ago, the night he turned up dead. It sounded to me like he was trying to warn you. Only someone who really cared would do that. You must have had him convinced that Joel was the red shoelace killer, because you knew Joel dated Jennifer Landis. But then your husband loves you, too, and that's why he did your bidding and came after us."

"I had Joel scared like a rabbit, too, and then he took up with you two, Fatso and Bubble Gum Brain."

I grabbed Rashawna's wrist when her nails were mere inches from Selena's face.

"When you realized Joel and Rashawna were dating, you had Joe abduct Rashawna. What were you going to do with her?"

Selena turned glittering black eyes on Rashawna. "We would have thought of something. Probably she wouldn't be standing here now with that fool look on her face." Then she spit on the ground.

I missed Rashawna's other wrist but grabbed it back before the second scratch.

Selena hardly seemed to feel it, but I saw her mammoth fist ball up. "You know, you weren't that hard to scare. A couple of red shoelaces in your car, and you're screaming like little girls. And you," Selena shot a withering glance at Joel, "even Joe thought you were the killer. It was all so perfect."

I shot a look at Rashawna. "You okay?"

"I'll be very okay when this one fries for murder." Her eyes narrowed, and she stared hard at Joe. Then she turned to Selena. "He's my abductor, and you had him grab me, didn't you? That's why he's got that bandage on his neck." She slowly turned and looked at Joe. "He's got a bad bruise on his head, too, but I didn't do that one."

"Some people are just real hard to kill," said Selena.

I realized suddenly what Selena had been carrying out of the Dollar Store the night before. Bandages. Joe's Rashawna-inflicted knife wound must have been a pretty nasty one. Not bad enough for him to stay holed up nursing it, though, unless someone else was with her then. Eddie?

There was a noise from the ground. Eddie sat up and rubbed his head. I was somewhat relieved that there wouldn't be a Taffy Tail kill to worry about in addition to everything else that had gone wrong that day.

"Where's my ..." Eddie looked at the scene before him, especially Joel, " ... gun. Never mind." He groaned and attempted to stand. Then he saw Joe and Selena.

"Hey, what are you guys doing here? Man, Joe, what happened to your head?"

Joel turned the gun on Eddie. "Sit down."

I looked at Joe. He wore a dark turtleneck shirt that covered most of the bandage on his neck, and the left side of his face had a dark ugly bruise that was spreading. He was slumped heavily against Selena now. She twisted her shoulders and grunted. "Why don't you just die?" She jerked her head viciously as a little sob escaped her lips.

Joe moaned and passed out. Now he was a dead weight against Selena, and her insane ranting continued.

"Eddie, if you'd just looked at me once," she sobbed, searching his face for some sign of concern.

Eddie gazed at her from a clueless fog. "I looked at you, Selena. Everybody looked at you, but I don't mess with my brother's wife."

"I'd have done anything for you. Every time I saw those girls laughing and running you down, I wanted to kill them. The meanest one, that Jennifer Landis, she deserved what she got."

"What are you talking about?"

"The Red Shoelace Killer is your sister-in-law," I said to Eddie.

Eddie shook his head to clear it and stared at Selena. "I always knew there was something a little off with you."

Just then my ears perked up to the sound of distant sirens, but there was one thing I wanted to find out from Eddie before Detective Horowitz and his crew got to us. "Did you follow us from the restaurant tonight?"

"You mean the rib place? I was there with my sister."

"Rashawna spoke with her," I said.

"Don't you get it?" yelled Selena. "Joe was my spy! He was following almost every move you idiots made. Even after the stab wound that Bubble Gum Brain gave him, I still made him dump that candy sack in your car. How dumb are you people, anyway?"

Selena seemed to be dissolving into a demented state.

"I didn't even know you were there. My sister was suddenly not feeling so good," said Eddie, "so we ordered some ribs to go and left the place about a half hour later. After I dropped her off at home, I came back to my own place and saw you guys creeping around."

"Where'd you get the gun?" Joel asked suspiciously.

Eddie laughed. "My nephew left it in my car. Its heavy-duty plastic, but it sure looks real, doesn't it? Has a little heft to it, too."

I felt myself go weak at the knees, and I thought Joel would faint, but he recovered quickly and slid his hand to the shotgun Rashawna had laid on the table.

"Where did you think you were taking us?" I asked.

"I just wanted to get you away from my restaurant," he said, shrugging. "I didn't want anybody finding these two at my place. Things are never what they seem with Selena around."

"No kidding," said Joel and Rashawna together.

It seemed Eddie wasn't completely clueless.

"I was on my way to dump him, Eddie." Selena's venting continued. She wanted Eddie to know all about her twisted love for him. "But he wouldn't die, he just wouldn't die, and then these idiots came along. Idiots!" She glared at Joel, Rashawna and me, spittle at the edges of her mouth. "I jumped into the truck beside Joe so they'd think we were both dead. I thought he was, but I guess I didn't hit him hard enough." She sighed heavily and sniffed. "Nothing ever works out for me."

In the next few moments the little park was flooded with light and just in time, too, as Selena gave up the battle to stay on the bench with her passed out husband, and they toppled onto the ground. Several police cars pulled into the kiddy park, and Detective Horowitz jumped out of one.

I hurried over to him. "Thank God you're here!"

"Minnie, nice to see you, too," he said, cool as a cucumber.

"I'm so glad you stayed on my cell line," I said, shaking with relief. "When he kidnapped us at gunpoint, I managed to punch four on my cell phone, and the idea did actually work, kind of."

"Looks like you've done all right on your own," Dan said. We watched as officers read the Miranda warning to Selena and Eddie. Joe was too far gone to respond, and I heard someone call for an ambulance. Dan turned to me. "Good work. Are you okay?"

"I'm … we're fine." I grinned at the praise, although getting abducted while skulking around Mack's Pier in the dead of night wasn't exactly my idea of sterling detective work.

"Minnie!" A beaming Rashawna click-clacked across the parking lot to me. "We caught him, Minnie, we caught him! Did you see me swing? Man, that sack of Taffy Tails was heavy."

I laughed. She had indeed been brave, and Joel, no less, for helping me keep the killer distracted. Joel stepped over to Rashawna's side.

"You are so my hero." She swiped playfully at his arm.

"Well, Minnie," said Detective Horowitz, "let me know if you ever want a part-time job in the department. You'll all come down and make statements in the morning, I'm sure." He winked at me and gave a little salute as he headed for his squad car.

"Okay, you two, time to head home." I motioned Joel and Rashawna toward my car. I was beginning to shiver badly and never wanted to leave a place so fast in my life.

"Minnie, we'd make a fine detective team, wouldn't we?" Rashawna said.

I laughed. "Sure, but right now all I want is a very hot cup of tea."

Twenty-Four

Rashawna and Joel did not stay with me that night, but they were at my door early the next morning with my favorite doughnuts and white chocolate lattes. A fitting start to the upcoming holiday season, I thought. We settled in at my kitchen table and tackled the goodies. Then we began to sort out our screwy week.

"I just don't get why they had to kill Roberto," said Rashawna.

"Joe was simply infatuated with Selena enough to blackmail her into marrying him," I said. "Stranger attractions have happened, but I think Roberto really loved her. He kept buying up all the red shoelaces with the mistaken idea that Joel would get them if he didn't."

"She must have had Joe do him in," said Joel. "Then he stole the blue truck, a real brassy guy."

"Except when it came to Selena," I said. "His bravado evaporated when it was about her." Something triggered in my brain just then. I got up and went over to my recliner. The day Briscoe and I had gone across the street to check out the blue truck, I'd written down the license plate number. I'd just remembered it was stashed in my recliner pocket. I pulled it out. Yup. BTO 843. Joe had been spying on us then, too.

"What's that, Min?" asked Joel.

I flashed the piece of paper. "Joe was the guy in the blue truck across the street a few days ago, and now I'm sure he was the one who followed me to the doughnut shop, too."

"That poor Roberto," said Rashawna, patting her chest with fluttering fingers. "He loved Selena from afar. Even with those cyst things on his forehead, he thought he had a chance."

"And he was trying to protect her from the killer by buying up all of the red shoelaces. He didn't want Selena to be the next victim. Unfortunately, he couldn't afford the gray sneakers with the red laces in that new shoe store."

"That's where Selena got the shoelaces to scare us with," said Rashawna.

"Mmm, I think she was saving those for her next two victims," I said. "They were very wide and about forty inches long."

"The two other girls remain clueless about it," said Joel. "I guess that's a good thing."

"Now the papers can let everyone know that it's safe, at least for now, for dark-haired young women to go out again," I said.

Joel ran two fingers down Rashawna's arm and leaned in. "Of course, I won't be letting you out of my sight," he cooed.

Rashawna let out a deeply contented sigh.

I looked at the doughnuts sitting in the middle of the table. Dare I take another? The white chocolate lattes were so good, I decided to savor mine and forgo another Boston crème.

"Roberto was as clueless as Eddie about Selena's true self," said Rashawna, "but Joe was crazy enough about her to kill his own cousin. How could so much evil be in one family?"

"People get strung out on emotions just like they do on drugs, and unrequited love can lead to all kinds of weird situations," I said. I hadn't read novel after novel and not found that out. "Poor Selena. As angry and troubled as she was, she still hoped to have a romantic relationship with Eddie."

"I don't think even Eddie would take up with an almost serial killer," said Rashawna.

"He'll probably have to close up the fish fry until this all blows over," said Joel.

I scooped a little whipped cream off the top of my drink as our conversation wound down. My phone rang just then. Dan Horowitz was calling to let me know that Joe had come out of surgery and would probably make a full recovery. Selena had slammed the side of his head with the butt of the rifle in her vicious attempt to do him in. Joe and Selena would be charged with a murder each, and aggravated assault would be added to Selena's charges for what she'd done to her husband—if he pressed for them, that is. Eddie would face lesser charges for abducting us and harboring fugitives. The red leather shoelaces from the All in Red shoe store had been found in Selena's truck, as well as the newspaper with the next victim marked. She'd finally found her token for the next red sweater girl. Fortunately, Selena would be in prison, and the other girls would be safe for now.

I filled Rashawna and Joel in on the situation. I could tell they were restless and eager to get on with their day and spend a few precious hours getting to know each other even better. Glenda had told us our bonus checks would be cut immediately, and the two lovebirds were soon off in Joel's ten-year-old BMW to collect theirs. I could wait until Wednesday, my regular day to check in at the Chapel Marketing office. I was pleased that I'd at least have enough to honor my pledge to the Christmas dinner at the Rescue Mission. It would make Briscoe feel proud to have gotten the commitment out of me.

Just before they left, Rashawna piped up, "Minnie, you asked about last night." She laced her arm through Joel's as they stood by my front door. "Joel drove me home, and you'll never guess who had come to visit: my Aunt Lucretia. My cousin Melinda and her little boy Clyde were there, too." She grinned up at Joel.

"That's wonderful, Rashawna," I said. "How long will they stay?"

"Just two days. They're all from New Jersey and just wanted to get away for a little while, so they came to see me. This year the leaves are so gorgeous, they'll love it. There's even a few small patches of snow for Clyde to play in."

"Yeah, after we drop Rashawna's bloody clothes off at the police station, we're taking the whole gang to the movies and dinner, maybe the rib place," said Joel, winking at me. "Gotta spend that bonus somewhere, right, Min?"

"Right," I said, "and they'll get to know you, too, Joel."

Rashawna hugged Joel's arm and opened the door. "My little cousin Clyde thinks Joel is wonderful. He's only four and loves to roughhouse." She was exuberant. "Have a good day Minnie!" And they were gone.

Twenty-Five

I was more than ready for a whole day of rest. Of course, that would have to include some shuffling of my summer clothes into the back of my closet and a few other mundane chores. It gave me time to ponder my Miss Marple-like experience of the past week. I had been beginning to think there were no more adventures in my life, and I'd just while away the days and weeks until I wound up nodding and drooling in whatever institution was found for me. But now I felt invigorated and began to see new possibilities for the years ahead.

"Hi, Deirdre," I said when I picked up the phone a few days later.

"Hi, Minnie," she answered. "No new projects yet. I just wanted you to know you can pick up your checks any time. They're here, and there's another bonus, too."

"Really," I said. "Whatever could that be?"

"Tell you when you get here," said Deirdre and rang off.

That afternoon I drove to the Chapel Marketing office. I was very pleased with my checks, and visions of fat sugarplums danced in my head.

"Wanna know the other bonus?" asked Deidre.

"You know I do," I said.

"Go on into the conference room."

I walked down to the room where we'd all learned about Brilliance Shampoo and was stunned to see dozens of boxes piled on the conference table. There had to be two cases each of every shampoo we'd pushed.

"Take as many as you'd like," said Glenda, who'd come in behind me.

"This is great," I said.

"The client was so pleased with our work, they sent these to every regional office."

"I guess there's a little Sybil in all of us," I said.

Glenda laughed. "Have a ball."

I took six bottles and figured that would last me a good long while. I couldn't wait for Rashawna to get a load of this deal. I wondered what our next project would be, but not too hard. It would come soon enough.

I left Chapel Marketing and looked forward to making myself a good lunch. After that I had the rest of the day ahead of me. Maybe I'd even take that sentimental journey in my lifetime room later in the day, then call and have a nice phone visit with my sister Maggie in Poughkeepsie. Really, I couldn't let all those free cell minutes lapse, now could I?

Meet Author Susan Sundwall

Susan calls home one of the most beautiful places on earth: Columbia County, New York. She and her husband live in a one-hundred-fifty year-old house on four lumpy, bumpy acres lined with pine trees. Her experience working as senior field manager for a local marketing company helped inform her first cross generation comic-cozy, The Red Shoelace Killer – A Minnie Markwood Mystery.

Susan would love to have you drop her a line at **susansundwall@gmail.com**? Or how about a visit to her website at **www.susansundwall.com** or blog at **www.susansundwall.blogspot.com** where there's always something going on!

CPSIA information can be obtained at www.ICGtesting.com
Printed in the USA
BVOW07s0532151214

379143BV00001B/23/P